LITTLE BOOK OF
FAIRY TALES

Retold by VERÓNICA URIBE

Translated by SUSAN OURIOU

Pictures by MURKASEC

GROUNDWOOD BOOKS
House of Anansi Press
TORONTO BERKELEY

First published in Spanish as EL LIBRO DE ORO DE LAS HADAS copyright © 2004 by Ediciones Ekaré, Caracas, Venezuela
First published in English by Groundwood Books
English translation copyright © 2004 by Susan Ouriou
Second printing 2006

Groundwood Books / House of Anansi Press
110 Spadina Avenue, Suite 801
Toronto, Ontario M5V 2K4
Distributed in the USA by
Publishers Group West
1700 Fourth Street, Berkeley, CA 94710

We acknowledge for their financial support of our publishing program the Government of Ontario through the Ontario Media Development Corporation's Ontario Book Initiative.

National Library of Canada Cataloging in Publication
Uribe, Verónica
Little book of fairy tales / retold by Verónica Uribe; pictures by Murkasec; translation by Susan Ouriou.
Translation of: El libro de oro de las hadas.
ISBN-13: 978-088899-583-4
ISBN-10: 0-88899-583-0
I. Ouriou, Susan II. Murkasec III. Title.
PZ8.U74Li 2004   J863   C2003-905018-1

The illustrations were done in Photoshop and Painter using a combination of photographs, drawings and scanned objects.

Art direction by Irene Savino
Printed and bound in China

TABLE OF CONTENTS

PUSS-IN-BOOTS

• AND THE MILLER'S SON •

Once there was a miller who died, leaving to his three sons a mill, a donkey and a cat as their only inheritance. The goods were shared out quickly. The eldest son inherited the mill, the second son the donkey, and the youngest son had to make do with the cat.

"My brothers will be able to earn a living with the mill and the donkey," the youngest son said to himself. "But what about me? Once I've eaten the cat and made a pair of gloves from its hide, I'll end up starving to death."

Although pretending to be asleep, the cat had been

listening. "Don't despair, Master," he said. "All you have to do is give me a sack and find me some boots to wear into the woods. Then you will see that your share of the inheritance is not as bad as it seems."

The miller's son looked at the cat and remembered how skillful he was at catching mice and rats in the mill by dangling his paws, ready to swipe at them from above, and how he played dead by burying himself in the flour. So he decided to give the cat a sack and a pair of boots.

The cat pulled on the boots then threw a fistful of wheat bran and some herbs into the sack. Flinging the sack over his shoulder, he ran to a place where he knew the rabbits were plentiful. Then he lay down on the ground, playing dead.

After a short while, a fat, careless rabbit approached, drawn by the smell of the herbs, and crawled into the sack. Puss-in-Boots pounced for the kill.

Then Puss-in-Boots proudly set off to request an audience with the king. He bowed low as soon as he was ushered into the royal chamber. "Sire," he said, "I have brought you a wild rabbit on behalf of and with greetings from his excellency the Marquis of Carabas."

"Give my thanks to your master, and tell him I am well pleased," the king said.

Another day, Puss-in-Boots hid in a field of wheat next to the open sack. This time he caught two partridges that he presented to the king, just as he had done with the rabbit.

•

Puss-in-Boots kept this up for two or three months, bringing his catch to the king and always telling him that it came with the compliments of the Marquis of Carabas. One day he heard of the king's plans to go on an outing along the riverbank with his daughter, the most beautiful princess in the world.

Puss-in-Boots ran back to his master, saying, "Follow my advice, and your future will be assured. You must go to the river to bathe. I'll show you the exact spot. Leave everything else up to me. Just remember, you are not the miller's son anymore, you are the Marquis of Carabas."

The miller's son did as Puss-in-Boots suggested. While he was bathing, the king's carriage passed by, and Puss-in-Boots began to shout, "Help! Help! My master the Marquis of Carabas is drowning!"

Hearing the cries, the king stuck his head out the carriage door and recognized the cat that had brought him so many gifts. He immediately ordered his footmen to rescue the marquis. Meanwhile, Puss-in-Boots approached the carriage and told the king that thieves had stolen his master's clothes while he was bathing. In fact, Puss-in-Boots had hidden the miller's son's humble clothes himself behind some bushes.

The king ordered his officers to bring one of his finest garments to give to the Marquis of Carabas.

The miller's son was gracious and polite and looked supremely handsome in the king's fine clothes. The princess took one look at him and fell madly in love. Seeing his daughter's happiness, the king invited the marquis to join them in their carriage.

Puss-in-Boots could not have been happier at the success of his plan. He set out ahead of the party, and seeing some workers harvesting a field of wheat, he stopped and said in a threatening tone, "The king will be by in his carriage any minute. When he asks who these fields belong to, you must tell him they belong to the Marquis of Carabas or he will make mincemeat out of you!"

And so it was. When the king asked to whom the bountiful fields belonged, the harvesters answered as one, "To the Marquis of Carabas!"

"You have an impressive estate, Marquis," the king remarked.

"Yes, Sire, I never fail to have a good harvest," the miller's son answered, beginning to understand what Puss-in-Boots was up to.

Puss-in-Boots kept walking on ahead. He met up with some vintagers harvesting clusters of grapes and said, "The king will be by shortly in his carriage. When he asks who the vineyard belongs to, you must tell him it belongs to the Marquis of Carabas or he will make mincemeat out of you!"

When the king drove by in his carriage and asked who the vines belonged to, the vintagers replied as one, "To the Marquis of Carabas, Sire!"

The king congratulated himself on being in the company of a marquis who owned so much land.

Puss-in-Boots continued on his way. He reached a beautiful castle which, like the land and cultivated fields so admired by the king, belonged to a terrible ogre.

Puss-in-Boots had taken pains to inquire about the ogre as he hunted rabbits and partridges for the king, and he knew what the ogre's magical powers were. Puss-in-Boots asked to see the ogre and explained, with great deference, that being this close to the castle, he felt he must stop in and pay his respects. The ogre was pleased.

"I've been told you have the power to change yourself into different animals," said Puss-in-Boots. "A lion or an elephant, for example."

"That I can," said the ogre gruffly. "You can see for yourself."

Zap! The ogre disappeared, and a huge lion with yellow eyes and sharp eyeteeth appeared.

In his fright, Puss-in-Boots scrambled up an eaves-trough all the way to the roof. But the ogre changed back almost immediately, pleased as punch to see the cat trembling in his boots.

"What a scare you gave me!" Puss-in-Boots confessed, once he had clambered back down. "But someone told me you can change yourself into small animals, too, a rat or mouse, for example. Now I have a hard time believing that. In fact, it sounds impossible."

"Impossible?" said the ogre with a disdainful smile. "You'll see."

Zap! The ogre changed into a tiny mouse and scurried past the cat.

Puss-in-Boots did not waste a second. He pounced on the mouse and gobbled it up. Just then the king and his party arrived at the castle. Puss-in-Boots went to meet them. He bowed low and said, "Sire, welcome to the castle of his excellency, the Marquis of Carabas."

"Indeed, Marquis!" the king exclaimed. "So this

castle belongs to you as well? I would love to be given a tour of this fine dwelling."

They stepped out of the carriage and entered the castle. Puss-in-Boots made his way to the kitchen where he ordered a sumptuous meal and the best wines. All was ready just as the others finished touring the castle and its gardens.

The king ate and drank to his heart's content, then he proposed to the marquis that he take his daughter's hand in marriage.

The Marquis of Carabas said he would be thrilled to accept the honor bestowed on him by the king. And the princess raised no objections, since she was madly in love with the marquis. They celebrated their engagement that very day and were married not long after.

Puss-in-Boots became a great lord and never had to hunt mice again, other than to amuse himself.

LITTLE RED
RIDING HOOD
• AND THE BIG BAD WOLF •

O nce upon a time there was a sweet, charming little girl who was as pretty as could be. Her mother was crazy about her and her grandmother even more so. She looked beautiful in whatever she wore, and her grandmother loved sewing lace-trimmed dresses and embroidering blouses and handkerchiefs for her.

One day the little girl's grandmother had a red riding cape made for her. The little girl loved the cape so much that she never took it off. And so she became known as Little Red Riding Hood to one and all.

One day, Little Red Riding Hood's mother called to her and said, "Your grandmother isn't well. Take her some homemade cake and a bottle of wine. But remember, don't stray off the path, don't skip — or you will break the bottle — don't forget to greet your grandmother when you arrive, and don't go poking all around."

"Don't worry, Mama. I'll be good," Little Red Riding Hood said and wished her mother good-bye.

Her grandmother lived deep in the woods. Halfway to her grandmother's house, Little Red Riding Hood ran into a wolf. He greeted her with a great big smile.

"Good day, Little Red Riding Hood."

"Good day, Mr. Wolf," she replied without fear, because she did not know what a bad wolf he was.

"Where are you off to so early?" the wolf asked.

"I'm going to see my grandmother."

"What do you have in your basket?"

"Some cake and a bottle of wine to help my grand-mother get better."

"Where does your grandmother live, Little Red Riding Hood?" the wolf asked.

"In the woods. Her house is under the three big oak trees."

The wolf fell into step with Little Red Riding Hood, wondering how he could treat himself, not only to the little girl, but to her grandmother as well. Finally he said, "Aren't the woods pretty? Look at all the wild roses in bloom! Listen to the little birds singing! You're in such a hurry. It's not like you're on your way to school! You're missing all the sights and sounds. There's such a lot to discover here in the woods if you take the time to stop and look."

Little Red Riding Hood opened her eyes wide and saw the way the sunbeams danced among the trees, and how there were flowers everywhere. She thought to herself, "My grandmother would love a bouquet of flowers. It's early yet. I'll still be there in plenty of time." And she turned off the path.

She wandered deeper into the woods looking for the prettiest flowers while gathering hazelnuts and chasing after butterflies. "The woods really are beautiful," she thought to herself.

Meanwhile, the wolf raced toward the grandmother's house. Once there, he knocked on the door. Tap! Tap!

"Who's there?" the grandmother asked.

"Little Red Riding Hood," the wolf said, disguising his voice. "I've brought you some cake and some wine. Let me in."

"I'm too weak to get up. Just pull on the cord to lift the doorlatch."

The wolf found the cord and pulled and the door opened. Without a word, the wolf crept over to the grandmother lying in bed and swallowed her whole.

Then he put on her nightdress and nightcap, drew the curtains around the bed and lay down.

Meanwhile, Little Red Riding Hood was happily exploring the woods. By the time she had gathered almost more flowers than she could carry, she remembered her errand and started back down the path that led to her grandmother's house.

The sight of the open door surprised her. She stepped inside with a vague sense of dread. Stopping at her grandmother's bedside she said, "Hello, Grandmother."

No answer. She opened the curtains and saw her grandmother wearing her nightcap. She looked so strange, not at all like herself.

"Oh, Grandmother, what big ears you have!" Little Red Riding Hood exclaimed.

"The better to hear you with," said the wolf, disguising his deep voice.

"Oh, Grandmother, what big eyes you have!"

"The better to see you with."

"Oh, Grandmother, what long arms you have!"

"The better to hug you with."

"Oh, Grandmother, what big teeth you have!"

"The better to eat you with."

With this, the wolf jumped out of bed and gobbled up Little Red Riding Hood. His stomach was so full that he lay back down, fell fast asleep and began to snore.

A hunter who happened to be passing by heard the wolf's horrible snoring and thought, "How strange for the grandmother to snore so loudly. I should check on her."

He stepped inside the house and saw the wolf asleep in the grandmother's bed. "You rotten wolf! At last, you're mine!" The hunter raised his shotgun, ready to fire, but then he thought better of it. Quietly, he picked up a pair of scissors and — snip, snip — slit open the wolf's belly. With the first snips, out jumped Little Red Riding Hood.

"It was so dark in there!" she cried.

Then out came her grandmother.

All three went looking for rocks to put in the wolf's belly before sewing him back up. When the big bad wolf awakened and saw the hunter, he jumped up, But his belly weighed him down so much, he stumbled and fell down dead.

The hunter skinned the wolf and took the hide away with him. The grandmother ate a piece of cake, drank a glass of wine and felt much better.

Little Red Riding Hood thought to herself, "If only I had stayed on the path, none of this would have happened."

SLEEPING BEAUTY
• IN THE WOODS •

Long, long ago there lived a king and queen who lamented day after day, "Oh, if only we had a child! How wonderful it would be to have a child!" Yet they never did.

But then one morning, when the queen was bathing, a toad jumped out of the water and said, "Your wish will be granted. Before the year is up, you will bring a child into the world."

•

And so it came to be. The next spring, the queen gave birth to a baby girl. The baby was so beautiful and the king was so happy that they decided to host a great feast in the castle. They invited all their relatives, friends and acquaintances from near and far, and they decided to invite all the fairies of the kingdom as well. As far as the king and queen could remember, there were seven fairies in all. Each one received an invitation.

The feast was a splendid celebration, and as the evening drew to a close, the fairies bestowed their wonderful gifts on the little girl.

The first fairy told her she would be the most beautiful woman in the world.

The second told her she would have an angel's soul.

The third told her that everything she did would be full of grace.

The fourth told her she would be a divine dancer.

The fifth told her she would sing like a nightingale.

The sixth told her she would make beautiful music, whatever instrument she played.

Just as the seventh fairy was about to speak, an old woman dressed all in black entered the castle, banging her wooden cane on the floor with each step she took.

The whole assembly fell silent, horrified. The old woman was the oldest fairy in the kingdom. She lived in an old secluded tower, deep in the forest. The color drained from the king's and queen's faces. They had forgotten to invite her!

"I see the oldest fairy in the kingdom is forgotten by all," the old woman said in a cracked, venomous voice. "This time, I will make sure no one ever forgets me again."

She limped over to the princess's cradle and whispered, "On the day you turn fifteen, you will prick your finger on a spindle and die."

Without another word, she turned on her heel and left the castle. For a moment, not a word was said in the huge throne room. Then the last of the seven fairies stepped forward.

"I cannot undo the oldest fairy's curse, but I can sweeten it. On the day you turn fifteen, dear princess, you will prick your finger on a spindle, but you will not die. You will fall into a sleep so deep, it will last one hundred years. Only a king's son will be able to awaken you."

The evening was over. Weeping, the queen gathered the princess into her arms and carried her to her apartments.

The king commanded that all spindles in the kingdom be burned. Then he published an edict banning all his subjects, whatever their station in life, from owning or using a spinning wheel or a spindle on pain of death.

Years passed and the princess grew more beautiful and charming by the day. Little by little, the king and queen forgot the old fairy's prophecy.

However, on the day of the princess's fifteenth birthday, while everyone was busy preparing for the celebration, the princess decided to explore the castle — every room, nook and cranny, inside and out.

From the garden she followed a path to an old tower she had never noticed before. She climbed up the narrow winding staircase and reached a small door that had a rusty key in the keyhole. When she turned the key, the door opened onto a tiny room in which an old woman sat spinning flax into cloth, using a spindle and spinning wheel.

"Good day, old woman," the princess said, then peered in surprise. "What are you doing?"

"Spinning flax," the old woman replied.

"Spinning? How wonderful! Could I try? What is this that bobs up and down so gaily?"

"This? A spindle, my dear," the old woman replied.

The princess reached out to take the spindle and pricked her finger instantly. No sooner had the first drop of blood appeared than the princess collapsed onto the bed and fell into a deep sleep.

Although nothing had been said by the seventh fairy, everyone in the castle fell asleep as well. The king and queen slept in the royal parlor, as did the courtiers and the orchestra musicians. The horses fell asleep in the stable, as did the dogs in the courtyard and the doves on the roof. The fire stopped crackling in the hearth, the roasting spits ground to a halt and the pots stopped boiling. The cook dozed off holding a ladle in his hand, his assistant holding a knife for peeling potatoes, and a woman fell fast asleep as she was plucking a hen.

Even the wind died down. Not a leaf stirred in the trees outside the castle.

Around the castle a huge hedge of thorn bushes began to grow. It grew bigger by the day until it completely hid the whole castle. Only the tallest turrets and their banners could be seen through the jungle of thorns. The legend of Sleeping Beauty of the Woods swept through the land. From time to time, young men tried to reach the castle to gaze on the sleeping princess. But one after another they gave up, discouraged by the hedge of fierce thorns that refused to give way under even the sharpest swords. Soon no one ventured into the woods anymore.

●

One hundred years passed. One day a king's son hunting nearby was intrigued by the turrets he glimpsed above the dense thicket. He asked people thereabouts what they were. Each person had a different story — that it was an old castle haunted by ghosts or a witch's castle or a fierce ogre's abode.

But one old man remembered the legend of Sleeping Beauty and told him that inside the castle the most beautiful princess in the world slept, waiting for the long-promised king's son to awaken her.

The prince did not hesitate for a second. He unsheathed his sword to clear himself a path, but found he did not need it. Beautiful flowers sprang up where the thicket had been and parted to let him through.

Stepping into the courtyard, he was greeted by the sight of the hunting dogs fast asleep, just like the horses in the stable and the doves on the roof. In the kitchen, he saw the woman frozen as she was about to pluck the hen, the cook with the ladle in his hand and his assistant holding the knife for peeling potatoes. Everyone was fast asleep. In the throne room, he saw

the king and queen, all the courtiers and the musicians sound asleep.

He did not stop there. The silence was such that he could hear himself breathing. The whole scene was so bizarre he did not know whether to be frightened or amused. He walked through the garden up to the tower and followed the narrow winding staircase up to the garret room where Sleeping Beauty had fallen asleep. He opened the door.

There she lay. She slept peacefully. The soft afternoon light shone on her hair, loose on the pillowcase, on her rose-colored cheeks and on her half-open lips. She was so beautiful he could not take his eyes off her. He leaned over and kissed her.

No sooner had his lips touched her own gentle lips than she opened her eyes, smiled, stretched and said, "What took you so long, my prince?"

They came down from the tower together and

walked toward the castle. As they approached, a gentle breeze began to blow. The doves shook out their feathers, the dogs wagged their tails and the horses whinnied in the stable. In the kitchen, the fire sprang to life, the roasting spit began to turn again and the pots returned to a boil. The cook woke up with the ladle in his hand, and so did his assistant with the knife. The woman began to pluck the hen, and a few flies resumed crawling up the wall. In the throne room, the entire court awoke at the same time as the king and the queen.

Since everything was already in place for a celebration — even the musicians — the king's son married Sleeping Beauty that very same night, and they lived happily ever after.

CINDERELLA
• AND THE
LITTLE GLASS SLIPPER •

Once there was a good man who lived happily with his wife and only daughter. But one day, his wife fell ill. Realizing that death was near, she called her daughter to her. "Don't be sad," she said. "I will always watch over you from heaven."

Then she closed her eyes and died.

Her daughter shed many a tear over her mother's death and kept her memory alive. One day she planted the twig of an almond tree at her mother's grave and watered it with her tears. When winter came, the snow blanketed the grave, and when the spring sun melted the snow away, her father took another wife.

His new wife was haughty and vain. Once the wedding was over, she let her bad temper show. Her two daughters came with her and were like her in every way.

From the moment the new wife set eyes on her husband's child, she hated her, for the young girl's sweetness and goodness underscored her own daughters' failings.

She made the girl cook, sweep and scrub and carry out all the menial chores around the house. She made her sleep in the barn on a straw mattress, while her own daughters were given the finest rooms with feather beds and tall mirrors. She took away her nice dresses, replacing them with a gray apron and a pair of wooden shoes.

Since a good part of the young girl's day was spent by the chimney, her apron and hands were covered in ashes and cinders. The sisters started to call her Cinderella.

"Look at the lovely cinder princess! Look at Cinderella!" they jeered at her.

The young girl endured their taunts without a word of complaint. When her work was done, she went to her mother's grave and watered the almond twig, which had begun to sprout roots and grow flowers.

•

It so happened that the king decided to host a ball to which he invited all the maidens of the kingdom, so that his son could find a bride among them.

The two sisters rejoiced at the news and immediately had the finest dresses and shoes made for themselves. They were too excited to eat. All they could do was talk about the ball and gaze at themselves in the mirror.

On the day of the ball, they asked Cinderella to

style their hair into two rows of curls, to fasten their dresses and to put on their bracelets and necklaces.

Cinderella helped them in every way. When the stepsisters were about to leave for the ball, she screwed up her courage and asked if, perhaps, she could go, too.

"You, Cinderella?" one of them said. "You're covered in dust and ashes, and you want to go the king's palace?"

"You have no clothes or shoes, and you want to go dancing?" said the other.

"That's out of the question," said her stepmother. "You would disgrace us all."

And they left.

Cinderella watched them until they were out of sight. Then she ran to her mother's grave and began to cry. She was weeping as though her heart would

break, when she heard a voice say, "Would you like to go to the ball, Cinderella?"

She dried her eyes and was astounded to see a fairy standing next to her.

"I would love to go to the ball," she said, with a sob. "But who are you?"

"I am your fairy godmother, and if you want to go to the ball, we have work to do. Go fetch me a pumpkin."

Cinderella ran to the garden and brought back a huge pumpkin. The fairy scooped it out, and when there was nothing left but the hollow shell, she gave it a tap with her magic wand. Immediately, the pumpkin turned into a beautiful gilded carriage.

"Now," said the fairy, "I need six mice."

Cinderella ran to fetch the mousetrap. She lifted the trap door, and the fairy tapped the mice with her wand as they ran past, turning them into fine showy horses.

"We still need a coachman," the fairy said.

"Maybe there's a rat in the rat trap," Cinderella replied.

There was indeed, a big fat rat with whiskers. The fairy tapped him with her wand and turned him into a stout coachman sporting a large moustache.

"Now fetch me three lizards behind the watering pail."

Cinderella ran to do her bidding, and when the fairy tapped the lizards with her magic wand, they turned into three elegant footmen who climbed up behind the coach, perching there as though they had done nothing else their entire lives.

"Well, now you have everything you need to go to the ball," said the fairy.

"Yes, that's true," said Cinderella. "But how can I go dressed like this?"

She pointed at her apron, all gray from the ashes.

"You're right," said the fairy, and she tapped Cinderella with her magic wand. In the blink of an eye, Cinderella's rags were transformed into a gorgeous red dress, and on her head appeared an elegant wig of soft white curls.

"There is still something missing," the fairy said, and she tapped Cinderella's wooden shoes with her wand. The shoes vanished and in their place appeared two lovely little glass slippers, the most beautiful slippers in the world.

Cinderella climbed into the coach. Her fairy godmother warned her that she had to return by midnight, because the spell would be broken when the clock struck twelve. Cinderella promised to leave by midnight. She was so happy to be going to the prince's ball.

When the gilded coach pulled up in front of the palace, the prince himself came out to greet her. He gave Cinderella his hand and escorted her into the ballroom, where all the guests were assembled.

Everyone fell silent as they entered. The dancing ceased and the violins stopped. All eyes were on the radiant beauty of the unknown princess. Murmurs spread from guest to guest. "She's so beautiful!" they said.

When the music started up again, the prince led Cinderella onto the dance floor. She danced so gracefully, he couldn't tear himself away from her. During the banquet, the prince did not even touch his food. He had eyes only for Cinderella.

The sisters' eyes were on Cinderella as well, but they did not recognize her. Cinderella went over to them and shared the oranges the prince had given her. Just then, she heard the clock strike a quarter to twelve. She curtsied and took her leave.

She ran from the palace and found her fairy god-

mother waiting for her at the house. Cinderella thanked her, telling her how much she would love to return to the palace the next day, since the prince had invited her back.

By the time the sisters got home, the carriage, the footmen, the coachman and the horses had disappeared. Cinderella was back in her worn apron and wooden shoes. She opened the door yawning and rubbing her eyes, as though she had just woken up, and asked them about the ball.

"If you had been there, you would have seen a mysterious princess, the most beautiful princess ever," one of the sisters said.

"She was very nice to us. She spoke to us and gave us some of her oranges," the other sister said.

Cinderella was happy at what she heard, and she asked for the princess's name. But they told her no one knew her name, although the king's son was clearly taken with her, and would give anything to find out who she was.

Cinderella smiled and asked, "Was she really that beautiful? You are so lucky to have seen her. Maybe I could go with you tomorrow to meet her?"

The stepsisters laughed. "You? Don't be crazy. We've already told you, you can't go to the king's palace."

And off to bed they went.

The next evening, as soon as the sisters left for the ball, Cinderella ran to her mother's grave to meet her fairy godmother. With a touch of her magic wand, her godmother made the carriage, the footmen, the coachman and the horses appear. Last of all, she tapped Cinderella's apron and turned it into a dress that was even more beautiful than the one she had worn the night before. As Cinderella left, her fairy godmother reminded her that the spell would be broken at midnight, and she must return before then.

The prince was waiting for her at the entrance to the palace and did not leave her side for a second. He danced with her and whispered tenderly in her ear.

Cinderella was so happy listening to him that she forgot her godmother's warning. When she heard the first stroke of midnight, she remembered the spell was about to be broken. Without even bidding the prince goodnight, she fled from the ballroom and ran down the staircase. But she was in such a hurry, she lost one of her lovely little glass slippers on the way.

The prince ran after the beautiful stranger, but by the time he got outside, all he could find was the little glass slipper. The prince picked it up and kept it.

Cinderella arrived home out of breath, without a carriage or footmen, wearing her dirty apron. Nothing remained of her recent splendor other than one of the little glass slippers, the mate to the one she had lost.

When the two sisters returned from the ball, Cinderella asked if they had enjoyed themselves as much as the previous night, and if they had seen the beautiful stranger again. They said yes, but that she had fled when the clock struck midnight and, in her hurry, had lost one of her lovely little glass slippers. The king's son had picked it up, and for the rest of the ball had done nothing but stare at it. They said there was no doubt he was much in love with the beautiful princess to whom the slipper belonged.

•

They spoke the truth because, a few days later, to the flourish of trumpets, the prince proclaimed that he would marry the woman whose foot fit the little glass slipper.

All the princesses, the duchesses, the countesses

and the ladies of the court tried the slipper on. But the little slipper fit none of their feet. So the prince ordered that all the maidens of the land should try it on.

The king's footmen took the slipper from house to house. When they arrived at Cinderella's house, the two sisters tried to force their feet into the slipper every which way, but in vain. Cinderella, who was watching, asked, "May I try it on?"

The two sisters burst out laughing, but the king's envoy looked intently at Cinderella, seeing how beautiful she was beneath her tattered clothes. He said it was his duty to try the slipper on all the maidens of the land and that, yes, she could try it. He asked Cinderella to sit down and watched with amazement as the slipper slipped on with no effort whatsoever, as though it had been made for her.

The sisters could not believe their eyes. They nearly

fainted with astonishment when they saw Cinderella pull the other slipper from her apron pocket and put it on, too.

At that, Cinderella's fairy godmother appeared. She tapped Cinderella's clothes with her magic wand, turning them into a dress even more magnificent than the one before. The king's envoy escorted her to the palace, where the prince thought her more beautiful than ever. A few days later, they were married.

Cinderella was so happy that she soon forgot how her sisters had mistreated her. She invited them to live with her in the king's palace, where they eventually married two lords of the court.

RUMPELSTILTSKIN
• THE LITTLE DANCING MAN •

Once upon a time there lived a poor miller who had a beautiful daughter.

One day he was obliged to ask for an audience with the king. Since he was nervous and wanted to make himself seem important, he said, "I have a daughter who can spin straw into gold."

The king answered, "That is a rare and delightful art. If what you say is true, bring your daughter to the palace tomorrow. I want to see how she fares."

The next day, the peasant brought his daughter with him. The king led her to a room full of straw, gave her a spinning wheel and spindle and said, " If all this straw has not been turned into gold by tomorrow morning, you shall die."

Then he himself bolted the door on his way out, leaving the girl alone inside.

The miller's daughter could not think what to do. She had no idea how to spin straw into gold, and did not understand why her father had got her into such a terrible fix. She felt so miserable and frightened that she began to cry.

Suddenly, out of nowhere, a little man appeared in the middle of the room and said, "Good afternoon, little miller's girl. Why are you weeping so?"

"Poor me," the girl replied. "I have to spin all this straw into gold, and I don't know how."

"What will you give me if I do it for you?" the little man asked.

The most valuable thing the young girl could think

of was the necklace she wore, and without hesitation she said, "My necklace."

The little man took her necklace and sat behind the spinning wheel. Whirr, whirr, whirr, three times round, and the straw turned into a fine skein of pure gold. He took a second bundle of straw and whirr, whirr, whirr, three times round, another glittering golden skein appeared. And so it went all night until all the straw had been spun, and the room was full of the most beautiful skeins of gold.

At daybreak, the king arrived. When he saw all the gold he was very pleased, but he was greedy for more. He took the miller's daughter into a bigger room full of straw, and ordered her to spin the straw into gold overnight if she valued her life. He closed the door and locked it.

Once more, the girl found herself alone in the room, and she began to cry. As soon as her face was awash with tears, the strange little man appeared out of nowhere.

"I don't like seeing a young girl cry," he said, then asked, "What will you give me now, little miller's girl, if I spin all this straw into gold?"

The girl remembered the ring her mother had given her on her fifteenth birthday and without hesitation said, "This ring."

The little man took her ring and sat down behind the spinning wheel. He began to turn the wheel, whirr, whirr, whirr, three times round, and the straw turned into fine skeins of gold. By daybreak, the work had been completed. The room was aglitter, and the young girl was relieved. The little man disappeared as silently as he had come.

The king arrived straightaway and rejoiced at the sight of the huge pile of gold, but still he wanted more. He took the miller's daughter into an even bigger room, it, too, full of straw, and repeated his order. "By daybreak tomorrow, all this straw must be spun into gold. If you succeed, you shall be my wife."

The young girl was left alone. She was not as frightened as before, but as the day wore on, the bundles of straw looked bigger and bigger. No matter how hard or how often she tried to turn the wheel, whirr, whirr, whirr, just like she had seen the little man do, the straw remained straw.

When night fell, she despaired and began to cry. As soon as her face was awash with tears, the little man appeared for the third time and said, "What will you give me now, little miller's girl, if I spin your straw again?"

"As you can see," the young girl answered hopelessly, "I have nothing of value left. I have nothing to give you."

"You may not have anything now," said the little

man, "but you will. Promise me that when you are queen, you will give me your firstborn."

The miller's daughter thought to herself, "Who knows what the future will bring?" In her despair, and not knowing what else to do, she accepted the little man's offer. For the third time, he spun the straw into gold.

At daybreak, the king returned and saw that everything was as he had hoped. Preparations for the wedding began, and the miller's beautiful daughter became queen.

●

A year went by, and the queen gave birth to a strapping baby boy. She was happy and had completely forgotten about the strange little man. But one night, he appeared in her room out of nowhere, while she was rocking the cradle and softly singing a lullaby.

The queen took fright at the sight of the little man.

He stood stiffly in front of her and said, "Give me what is mine."

"Oh, no, I can't!" the queen exclaimed. "I can't give you my son. But I have all kinds of riches now. They are yours for the asking."

"I prefer something living and tender to all the riches in the world," the little man said shrilly.

The queen was heartbroken. She begged and pleaded, but the little man insisted she keep her promise. Devastated at the thought she would never see her son again, the queen began to cry. When her face was awash with tears, the little man softened.

"I don't like to see a queen cry, either," he grumbled. Then he added, "I give you three days to find out my name. If by the end of the three days you are able to tell me what my name is, you can keep your son."

And he disappeared.

The queen spent all night trying to think what the strange little man's name might be, and finally decided his name must be as strange as he was.

Early the next morning, she sent a messenger to travel through the land asking people for the most unusual names they had ever heard.

The messenger memorized the names and repeated them to the queen, who jotted down each and every one.

When the little man came back that night, the queen said, "Caspar."

"That is not my name. No and no again."

"Melchior."

"That is not my name. No and no again."

"Balthasar."

"That is not my name. No and no again."

"Damoscene."

"That is not my name. No and no again."

Each time he said no and no again, the little man danced on one foot and rubbed his hands in glee.

The queen read out all the strange names she had jotted down, until not one was left. None of them was the little man's name.

"I'll be back tomorrow night," he said, then disappeared.

Now the queen thought to herself that the little man's name must be a simple, well-known name, and she prepared a new list.

When the little man arrived that night, she said, "John."

"No, no way. That is not my name."

"Peter."

"No, no way. That is not my name."

"James."

"No, no way. That is not my name."

"Matthew."

"No, no way. That is not my name."

Every time the little man said no, no way, he danced on one foot and rubbed his hands in glee.

The queen kept reading from her long list of common names, but none of them was his.

"Tomorrow is the last night," he said. "You must guess my name, or I will take your son away."

The desperate queen sent her messenger through the land once more to gather all the names, simple or strange, old or new, and bring them to her before sundown.

The messenger came back that night, tired and covered in dust from all the roads he had traveled. He said to the queen, "Nothing, my lady. I haven't come up with a single name other than the ones I already gave you."

"Not a single one? Are you sure?"

"Only that...when I rounded a bend through the

woods, in a dark place rarely touched by the sun, I saw a small cottage, and in front of the cottage a blazing fire and a ridiculous little man dancing around the fire. He was rubbing his hands together, laughing, dancing on one foot, and singing this song:

TOMORROW I DANCE, TODAY I SING,
SOON THE CHILD IS MINE TO BRING.
OH WHAT LUCK TO WIN THIS GAME,
RUMPELSTILTSKIN IS MY NAME.

"That's it!" the queen exclaimed.

That night when the little man appeared, she said, "Might your name be Henry?"

"No and no again."

"What about William?"

"No and no again," the little man answered, rubbing his hands together in glee.

"Then it must be Rumpelstiltskin, the little dancing man," the queen said.

The little man was furious. "Only the devil could have told you," he shouted. "No one knows my name! Oh! Oh! How infuriating!"

Raging still, he stamped his foot so hard that he sank into the ground right up to his waist. And he kept stamping his feet, until the earth swallowed him whole.

Once again, the queen started to rock the cradle and sing lullabies to put her son to sleep. People say that she lived happily ever after and never saw the little dancing man again.

RAPUNZEL
• OF THE TOWER •

Once a man and a woman lived together in a small cottage. They were poor and the cottage was humble, but it had something special — a window looking onto a beautiful garden that belonged to the witch next door. The garden was surrounded by a high wall. No one could get into it to see its beauty.

The window was the only spot from which the flowering climbing vines, the many-hued roses, the orange trees in blossom, the delicate lilies and the water lilies, floating on the pond, could be enjoyed.

Past the flower garden was the vegetable garden.

The woman sat at the window every afternoon carefully keeping out of sight of her neighbor, the wicked witch, and felt happy. There was only one thing missing for her to know total bliss — a child.

Then one day she knew she was expecting a baby.

Her husband was delighted at the news and lavished affection on his wife. He did the heaviest work around the house and catered to her every need.

One afternoon, while the woman was gazing at the witch's garden, she saw some turnip plants. They looked so fresh, with tiny drops of dew on their leaves, that she felt an irresistible urge for turnip salad.

She called her husband and said, "Do you see that turnip in the garden? Doesn't it look tempting? Don't you think it would be delicious in a salad?"

"Have you gone out of your mind, woman? That's the witch's garden. No one is allowed inside."

His wife said nothing, but looked very sad. Her husband saw her staring silently at the turnip in the garden, and his heart softened. He climbed the high wall, and cautiously let himself down the other side to gather some turnip as quickly as he could.

His wife prepared a large salad, which she ate with great relish.

"Delicious!" she said, smiling. "Thank you, dear husband."

The next day, the woman sat down to gaze at the witch's beautiful garden. She noticed some yellow roses that had just come into bloom, she watched a dragonfly hover over the water lilies, and beyond that, in the vegetable garden, she spied some glossy red tomatoes.

She called out to her husband without thinking, "Do you see those tomatoes over in the vegetable garden? See how red and smooth they look? Don't you think they would make a delicious salad?"

"Woman, that's the witch's garden," the man reminded her.

"Alas, dear husband, I think I shall die if I don't taste those tomatoes."

The poor man could not bear to see his wife suffer, so he climbed the wall and cautiously let himself down the other side to the witch's garden where he quickly picked six tomatoes. He was about to turn back when he saw the witch towering over him.

"How dare you steal tomatoes from my vegetable garden! How dare you enter my flower garden!" she thundered.

The poor man was struck with terror, but he managed to speak. "My wife had a craving for the vegetables in your garden," he explained. "You see, she's expecting a child within a few months' time, and she told me she would die if she didn't have these tomatoes."

This seemed to satisfy the witch. "Fine," she said. "I won't kill or hurt you. Your wife will be able to eat anything she wants from my garden, and I will let you gather any flowers she would like. But when your baby is born, you must give it to me. I will take good care of it. It will want for nothing."

The frightened man agreed to the witch's terms.

When his wife gave birth to a beautiful little girl, the witch appeared. She took the baby into her skinny arms, gave her the name Rapunzel and took her away.

Rapunzel was the most beautiful child under the sun. When she turned twelve, the witch shut her up in a tower, deep in the woods. It was a very tall tower with no door or stairs, nothing but one small window up high.

Whenever the witch wanted to enter, she called out from below,

RAPUNZEL, RAPUNZEL,
LET DOWN YOUR GOLDEN HAIR.

Rapunzel's hair was as blonde and fine as spun gold. When she heard the witch's voice, she undid her braids and fastened them over a hook above the window, letting them fall to the foot of the tower. Clinging to her hair, the witch climbed up to Rapunzel's room.

Time passed.

One day, the king's son was out riding. He ventured into the dark woods, and by a clearing heard someone singing in a sweet, lonely voice. The gentle sound led him to the tower. Up high in the tiny window, he saw Rapunzel singing to herself. He felt a desperate urge to climb the tower to see the beautiful girl up close. But he could find no door or staircase, and had to give up.

He returned to the palace, but the sound of

Rapunzel's voice had so moved him that he returned to the woods every day just to hear it.

One day as he leaned against a tree, he saw the witch approaching and heard her cry,

RAPUNZEL, RAPUNZEL,
LET DOWN YOUR GOLDEN HAIR.

Rapunzel let her hair fall down, and the witch climbed up to the window.

"If that's the stairway to the top of the tower, I will climb it as well," thought the king's son.

The next day, as darkness fell, he approached the tower and shouted,

RAPUNZEL, RAPUNZEL,
LET DOWN YOUR GOLDEN HAIR.

Down came her hair, and the king's son climbed up.

Rapunzel was frightened when she saw the prince, since she had never set eyes on a man before. But the king's son spoke to her tenderly. He told her how her voice and her sweet melody had affected him so greatly, he had not known a moment's peace until just then, seeing her.

Listening to him, Rapunzel lost her fear, and when he asked if she would take him for her husband, she noticed how young and handsome he was. She thought, "He will love me more than the old witch does."

"Yes, I will," she said and put her hand over his. "I would gladly leave with you right away, but I don't know how to get out. Every time you come, bring a length of silk rope with you. I will make a ladder from it. When it is ready, the two of us will be able to climb down, and you will take me away on horseback."

Every evening, the prince came back to see Rapunzel. And every evening, he brought her a few lengths of silk rope.

The witch did not notice a thing, because she only visited the tower in the morning. But on one such morning, while the witch was making her laborious way up to the tower, Rapunzel muttered, "Oh, this old woman is so heavy and takes so long. Not like my beloved who takes no more than a minute to join me."

The old witch heard her words. "Impudent child! What is that I hear you say? I thought I had shut you off from the rest of the world, and you have deceived me."

And full of anger, the witch struck Rapunzel. Then she twisted her hair around her left hand, and with her right hand, grabbed a huge pair of scissors and — snip, snip — cut off Rapunzel's golden hair.

But her fury did not end there. She took Rapunzel to a barren desert where she abandoned her.

That evening when the king's son went to the tower, the witch hung Rapunzel's hair from the hook and threw it down. Not knowing what awaited him, the prince climbed up as usual. Instead of his sweetheart, he came face to face with the wicked witch, still furious.

"You'll hear no more songs from your lovely bird," she said. "And you will pay for your gall. No one who dares deceive a witch goes unpunished. Not only will you never hear Rapunzel again, you will never see her again either."

She threw him from the tower. The prince fell into a thorn bush and hundreds of thorns pierced his eyes, leaving him blind.

Many years passed. The king's son wandered aimlessly through the woods day after day, remembering Rapunzel's sweet song. Meanwhile, she wandered aimlessly over the hot sand of the desert, unable to forget the king's son. Every evening she sang her song to feel near him. One day her song was so sad, the wind gathered it up and carried it to the woods and the prince.

Once again, the prince followed the sweet voice of his beloved, until he reached her side. They embraced as before. Rapunzel wept on seeing him, and two of her tears fell on the prince's blind eyes. His eyes cleared, and his sight was restored.

The prince took Rapunzel back to his kingdom with him. They were never again separated and lived happily together for many, many years.

THE PEASANT'S CLEVER DAUGHTER
• AND THE KING'S RIDDLE •

Once upon a time there was a poor peasant who owned no land. All he had was a tiny house and an only daughter.

Seeing that they had nothing, his daughter, a very clever girl, said to her father, "Why don't you go to the king and ask him for some land, just a small parcel of land, so we can sow and reap crops?"

Her father followed her advice and, out of pity for the poor peasant, the king granted him a tract of land that had never been cultivated before.

The peasant and his daughter cleared the land, plowed it and sowed their crops. After some time, they were able to harvest their crops and lead a better life.

Several years went by and the peasant's daughter grew into a pretty young woman.

One day in the sowing season, they came upon a small mortar made of pure gold buried in a corner of their field.

"We shall take this to the king," the peasant said. "To show him how grateful we are for the land he gave us."

"Don't do that, Father," the girl said. "We have to find the pestle first. Don't say anything to the king yet."

But the peasant ignored his daughter and took the mortar to the palace. He asked to speak to the king and told him he had a gift for him, a gold mortar he had found. He begged the king to accept it as a token of his respect. The king took the mortar and asked him if he had found anything else.

"No, Sire," answered the peasant.

"How can that be?" the king asked. "You didn't find a pestle along with the mortar?"

"No," the peasant said again. "All I found was the mortar."

By then the king was furious. He ordered the man to be taken to prison, and fed nothing but bread and water, until he revealed where he had hidden the pestle.

The peasant bemoaned his fate loudly. "Woe is me! If only I had done as my daughter said. Woe is me! If only I had listened to her advice. Woe is me! If only I had paid attention to reason, I wouldn't be here, a prisoner, living on nothing but bread and water."

The guards heard him crying and wailing and told the servants. The servants told the cook, the cook told the valet and the valet told the king. The king ordered that the peasant be brought before him.

"Why do you cry so? Why do you say if only you had listened to your daughter?" the king asked.

"She's the one who told me not to bring you the gold mortar as a present unless I had the pestle as well."

"I see you have a very clever daughter," the king said. He ordered that she be brought to the palace.

When the young girl arrived, the king told her that he had heard she was very clever, and that he wanted her to solve a riddle.

"That I can do," the girl said, very sure of herself.

"We shall see," the king said. "You must come to see me neither clothed nor naked, neither riding nor in a carriage, neither on the road nor off the road. If you do, I will marry you."

The young girl went home and got undressed, and in this way she was not clothed. She took a fishing net and wrapped it around her, and in this way she was not naked.

She fetched a donkey and tied the end of the fishing net to its tail, and in this way she would be dragged by the donkey, neither riding nor in a carriage.

The donkey set off toward the palace, and the girl made sure to stay partly on the road and partly on the grass at the side of the road, and in this way she was neither on nor off the road.

This was how she reported to the king, who was greatly amused by the spectacle. "You have done what I asked," he said. "I will marry you."

He had her father freed from prison, took her as his wife and made her responsible for administering his estates.

Months and years went by and the king's wealth increased, thanks to the wise decisions made by his clever queen.

One day, the king was reviewing his troops when there was a disturbance in the middle of the square. Some woodcutters were fighting over a newborn foal.

One of the woodcutters had brought his load of wood to town in a cart pulled by a horse and a mare. The other woodcutter's cart was pulled by a pair of oxen. The foal had escaped and sought shelter between the two oxen. The owner of the oxen said the foal was his, because it had sought refuge between his oxen. The other woodcutter said the foal was his, because his mare had given birth to it.

They were about to come to blows when they decided to go to the king and ask that justice be done. The king decided the foal should stay where it was. The owner of the cart pulled by the oxen kept the foal, even though it was not his. The other woodcutter left crying.

He was walking home with a heavy heart when an

old woman told him he should go to see the queen. She had heard that the queen was compassionate, being the daughter of peasants herself. So the woodcutter did just that. He went to the queen and asked her to help him get his foal back.

"I will help you," said the queen. "But you must not tell anyone. Give me your word."

The woodcutter gave his word.

The next day he returned to the square in front of the palace and did what the queen had told him to do.

He stationed himself just below the balcony where the king could see him, and threw his fishing net several times, reeling it back in each time as though it was full of fish. He pretended to put the fish in his basket then threw the net again. The king saw him from the window and sent an emissary to ask what he was doing.

"I'm fishing," the woodcutter said.

"But there's no water. How can you be fishing?" the emissary asked.

"Just as two oxen can give birth to a foal, I can fish on dry land."

The emissary went back to the king and repeated what the woodcutter had said. His reasoning sounded familiar to the king, and he had the man brought straight to him.

"Who suggested you go fishing on dry land in front of my balcony?"

The frightened woodcutter answered, "No one, Sire, no one. God protect me!"

The king ordered him horsewhipped and after the first few lashes, the woodcutter confessed the suggestion had come from the queen.

The king was furious. He called his wife in and said, "How dare you mock my rulings? I no longer want you as my wife. Go back to where you came from."

The queen was greatly saddened at this and asked if they could not have one last meal together. The king consented. Seeing her eyes brimming with tears, he told her she could take home whatever she loved best from the palace as well.

The queen had a delicious meal prepared and the best wine brought in. Unknown to the king, she added to his glass three drops of an elixir that made him dizzy and sent him into a deep sleep. Once he was asleep, she called for the servants. It took several of them to put him in a fine white linen cloth and carry him to a carriage waiting at the door. The queen took him to her father's little house.

The king slept for two days and when he awoke, he asked, frightened, "Where I am? What is all this?"

He shouted for his servants, but there were none. The only person who came to the foot of his bed was his wife. "You? Have you disobeyed me?"

"Oh, no, dear husband. You ordered me to take what I loved best from the palace. Since there is nothing I love more than you, I brought you with me."

The king smiled, then burst into laughter.

"No one can outwit the king's clever wife," he said. Then he escorted her back to the royal palace.

SNOW WHITE

• AND THE
SEVEN LITTLE MEN •

Once upon a time in the middle of winter, when snowflakes fell like feathers, a queen sat sewing next to a window, its frame made of ebony. As she sewed and watched the snow fall, she pricked her finger with the needle. She opened the window, shook her hand and three drops of blood fell on the snow. The red was so beautiful against the snow that she thought to herself, "If only I had a daughter as white as snow, as red as blood and as black as the wooden frame of this window."

Not long afterward, she gave birth to a little girl as white as snow and as red as blood whose hair was as black as ebony. She named her Snow White.

After Snow White was born, the queen died.

A year passed and the king took another wife. She was a beautiful woman, but vain and arrogant, and she could not stand for anyone to be as beautiful as she. She had a magic mirror before which she stood every day and asked:

> MIRROR, MIRROR
> ON THE WALL
> WHO'S THE FAIREST
> ONE OF ALL?

The mirror always answered:

> YOU, MY QUEEN AND LADY,
> NONE IS FAIRER THAN THEE.

Then she was happy since she knew the mirror spoke the truth.

Time passed and Snow White grew. When she turned seven, she was as beautiful as a May morning and more beautiful than the queen. That day, as usual, the queen asked her magic mirror:

MIRROR, MIRROR
ON THE WALL
WHO'S THE FAIREST
ONE OF ALL?

The mirror answered:

MY QUEEN, YOU WERE THE FAIREST HERE,
BUT NOW MORE FAIR IS SNOW WHITE NEAR.

The queen thought she would faint. From then on, just the sight of Snow White made her ill. Envy and arrogance grew in her heart like weeds, and she found no peace neither night nor day.

One afternoon she called for the huntsman and said, "I never want to see Snow White again. Take her into the woods and kill her. Then bring her heart back to me."

The huntsman obeyed and took Snow White into the woods. He had his hunting knife ready to plunge into the young girl's heart, when she cried, "Please let me go, dear Huntsman. I'll run deep into the woods and never come back again."

She was so beautiful and so fragile that the huntsman took pity on her and said, "All right, run away, poor child."

As Snow White ran off, the huntsman thought to himself, "The wild animals of the forest will eat you before long, but at least I won't have been the one to have killed you." When a young boar ran by, he stabbed it, removed its heart and carried it back to the queen as proof.

The queen was satisfied.

Meanwhile, Snow White ran and ran through the woods, skirting thorn bushes and rocks. She climbed seven mountains and crossed seven streams. Soon night fell, a dark, black night here in the woods. Snow White caught sight of a small cottage in the darkness and decided to venture inside to rest.

Everything inside the cottage was little. There was a little table covered with a white tablecloth and seven little plates, each plate with a little spoon, seven little knives and seven little forks, seven little glasses and seven little buns. There were also seven little beds with seven little snow-white sheets, seven little down quilts and seven little pillows.

Snow White was so hungry and thirsty that she sat down at the table and ate a little something from every plate — some vegetables and buns, a bit of custard and cheese, a sampling of rice and pheasant and, at the very last, a drop of wine from each little glass.

By then she was so tired, she decided to lie down. She tried each of the little beds in turn, but none of them was just right. One was too hard, the other was too soft, one was too cold, the other creaked, one was too firm, the other gave no support. Until, that is, she reached the last little bed and found it so much to her liking that she tumbled in, said her prayers and fell fast asleep.

●

Much later that night, the owners of the cottage returned home. They were seven little men who worked in the mines looking for gold and silver. They lit their seven little lamps and realized someone had been in their house.

The first little man said, "Who has been eating off my little plate?"

The second one said, "Who has been eating my little bun?"

The third one said, "Who has been eating my little rice?"

The fourth one said, "Who has been eating my little custard?'

The fifth one said, "Who has been pecking at my little vegetables?"

The sixth one said, "Who has been dining on my little pheasant?"

The seventh one said, "Who has been nibbling at my little cheese?"

Seeing their glasses, they all exclaimed together, "Who has been drinking our little wine?"

The oldest little man walked over to his bed, and seeing it was all wrinkled said, "Someone has been in my little bed."

The other little men checked their beds and exclaimed, "Someone has been in our little beds."

But the smallest little man of all said nothing. He

saw Snow White asleep in his bed and called the others over. They raised their little lamps for a good look at her and whispered together, "Oh, what a lovely girl. What shall we do with her? What indeed, what indeed?"

They decided to let her sleep until the next day when they asked her, "What is your name? Where do you come from? Why are you in our little house?"

So Snow White told them everything.

The little men told her that if she did the washing and ironing, the weaving and sewing, the cooking and cleaning, she could stay with them. Snow White answered, "I'd be happy to."

And she stayed with the little men.

Every morning the little men headed into the mountains to dig for silver and gold. They came home at dusk and expected the cottage to be tidy and the meal prepared. Snow White spent all day alone, and

the little men warned her as they left, "Don't open the door to anyone. Your stepmother might find out where you are."

●

Months then years passed. The queen had not bothered asking her mirror who was the fairest one of all again, since she was sure it was she. One day, however, she decided to ask once more:

MIRROR, MIRROR
ON THE WALL
WHO'S THE FAIREST
ONE OF ALL?

The mirror answered:

HERE YOU'RE THE FAIREST, MY DEAR QUEEN
BUT THE FAIREST OF ALL STILL LIVES ON
        UNSEEN
OUT IN THE WOODS SO FAR AWAY

SNOW WHITE IS THE FAIREST BY NIGHT AND
DAY.

The queen shuddered, knowing the mirror would
never lie. She realized that she had been deceived by
the huntsman, and that Snow White was still alive.
Once again, she was consumed by envy. She began to
make plans to kill Snow White. So long as the queen
was not the fairest of all, she would know no peace.

When she had finally decided what to do, she
painted her face and dressed as a peddler so no one
could recognize her. Off she went deep into the
woods. She climbed seven mountains and crossed
seven streams until she reached the cottage of the
seven little men.

"Pretty wares for sale!" she cried out, knocking on
the door.

Snow White peeked out the window and asked,
"What is it you're selling?"

"Some of the finest silk laces," said the queen, disguising her voice. "Let me in, and I will show you."

Snow White could see no danger in letting the peddler woman inside, and she unbolted the door. The queen entered and Snow White bought two corset laces from her, one blue, the other gold.

"Dear child, they suit you so well," the queen said, still disguising her voice. "I'll put them around your waist for you."

An unsuspecting Snow White let the queen put the new laces on, but the queen cinched them so quickly and so tightly that Snow White stopped breathing and fell over as though dead.

"Now I am the fairest one of all," said the queen and left.

At nightfall, the seven little men returned home and were greeted by the horrifying sight of Snow White lying motionless on the floor. They picked her up, and when they saw the laces cinched so tightly around her waist, they cut them off. Gradually, she began to breathe again and life was restored to her.

When the little men heard what had happened, they told her, "That woman can have been none other than the wicked queen. Be careful, you must not let anyone inside if we are not here with you."

Upon reaching the palace, the queen headed straight for the mirror and asked:

MIRROR, MIRROR
ON THE WALL
WHO'S THE FAIREST
ONE OF ALL?

Just as before, the mirror answered:

HERE YOU'RE THE FAIREST, MY DEAR QUEEN
BUT THE FAIREST OF ALL STILL LIVES ON UNSEEN
OUT IN THE WOODS SO FAR AWAY

SNOW WHITE IS THE FAIREST BY NIGHT AND DAY.

Hearing this, the blood rushed to the queen's head, and she shuddered at the thought that Snow White was still alive. "Fine," she said. "I must come up with an even better plan."

Knowing something of witchcraft, she made a poisonous comb. She disguised herself as an old woman and set off through the woods. She climbed seven mountains and crossed seven streams until she reached the cottage of the seven little men.

She knocked on the door and cried, "Pretty wares for sale!"

Snow White peeked out the window and said, "Go on your way, I can't let anyone in."

"At least have a look," the queen answered, disguising her voice, and she showed her the pretty comb.

Snow White liked it so much, she opened the door to the queen, in her old woman's disguise, and bought the comb from her.

"Now then, I shall comb your hair," the queen said, and suspecting nothing, Snow White let her.

As soon as the comb touched Snow White's hair, the queen jabbed it into her head and the venom did its work. Snow White fell senseless to the floor.

"Now I am the fairest one of all," the queen said and left.

Fortunately, night soon fell and the seven little men returned home. When they saw Snow White lying on the floor, they immediately suspected her stepmother and searched until they found the poisoned comb. No sooner had they pulled it out than Snow White came to, and told them what had happened. The little men scolded her and told her once again to be careful and not open the door to a single soul.

Back in the palace, the queen went to her mirror and asked:

> MIRROR, MIRROR
>
> ON THE WALL
>
> WHO'S THE FAIREST
>
> ONE OF ALL?

The mirror answered:

> QUEEN, THOU ART OF BEAUTY RARE,
>
> BUT SNOW WHITE LIVING IN THE GLEN
>
> WITH THE SEVEN LITTLE MEN
>
> IS A THOUSAND TIMES MORE FAIR.

Hearing this, the queen started to tremble with rage. "Snow White must die," she said.

She shut herself up in a dark forgotten room in which no one ever set foot and prepared a poisonous apple. On the outside it looked like a delicious apple

— half red, half white, fresh and tasty. But whoever ate a piece of the apple would die instantly.

The queen disguised herself as a peasant woman and walked into the woods. She climbed seven mountains and crossed seven streams until she reached the cottage of the seven little men, and knocked on the door.

Snow White looked out the window and said, "I can't let a single soul inside. The little men have forbidden it."

"That's all right," said the queen, disguising her voice. "But I brought too many apples with me. I would like to give you one. Here, have one."

"No," said Snow White. "I can't accept anything."

"Just try this one slice," said the queen, as she cut off a piece of the apple. "It's delicious."

Snow White knew she should resist, but the apple looked so juicy and appetizing that she reached out, took the slice the peasant woman handed her and bit into it. Instantly, she fell down dead.

The queen looked at her and said, "White as snow, red as blood, black as ebony. This time the little men won't be able to waken you."

Back at the palace, she asked the mirror:

> MIRROR, MIRROR
>
> ON THE WALL
>
> WHO'S THE FAIREST
>
> ONE OF ALL?

Finally, the mirror answered:

> YOU, MY QUEEN AND LADY
>
> NONE IS FAIRER THAN THEE.

The queen's envious heart was stilled.

When the little men returned home, they saw Snow White lying on the floor. Not a breath escaped from her lips. They picked her up, unlaced her corset, combed her hair, bathed her with water and wine, but all to no avail. The beautiful young maiden was dead and remained so.

They laid her on a white sheet and wept at her side for three days and three nights. Afterward, they thought they should bury her, but couldn't bring themselves to do so. She looked like she was just sleeping, her skin as soft and her cheeks as rosy as they had always been.

"We can't possibly put her into the cold ground," the little men said.

They built a glass coffin, so she could be seen from all four sides, and wrote "Snow White" in gold letters on it. They also wrote that she was the daughter of a king. They placed the coffin at the top of a gentle hill, in a clearing, and one of the little men stood guard over her at all times. Birds came and wept for Snow White — first an owl, then a raven and finally, a little dove.

Snow White lay in the coffin for a very long time as though asleep. She remained as beautiful as ever, as white as snow, as red as blood, with hair as black as ebony.

One day it so happened that a prince entered the wood, climbed seven mountains, crossed seven streams and reached the hill where Snow White lay. He saw the coffin and the beautiful maiden inside, read what was written in gold and said to the little men, "I'll give you whatever you would like for the glass coffin and the princess sleeping inside."

"We wouldn't sell it to you for all the gold in the world," the little men replied.

The prince insisted, and the little men refused once more. Snow White looked so calm and peaceful, as though asleep. The prince did not see how he could part from her.

"Give her to me then, I can no longer live without seeing Snow White."

Hearing his words, the little men felt sorry for him and gave him the coffin. The jubilant prince ordered his servants to carry it on their shoulders. But one of them tripped over a bush, knocking the coffin onto the ground.

Snow White was jolted by the fall, and the piece of poison apple that was stuck in her throat fell out. Snow White opened her eyes, lifted the top to the coffin and sat up. Once again, life had been restored to her.

"Where am I? Who are you?" she asked.

Bursting with happiness, the prince replied, "Don't be afraid. I will protect you. Come with me to my father's palace, and you will be my wife."

The idea pleased Snow White, and she left with him.

The wedding was a grand celebration with thousands of guests. One of them was the wicked queen, who had no idea who the beautiful princess betrothed to the prince really was.

The queen got dressed in her finest then stood in front of the magic mirror and asked:

MIRROR, MIRROR

ON THE WALL

WHO'S THE FAIREST

ONE OF ALL?

The mirror answered:

HERE YOU'RE THE FAIREST

BUT THE WORLD HAS NEVER SEEN

A WOMAN ANY FAIRER

THAN THE YOUNG NEW QUEEN.

The wicked woman's fury knew no bounds. She stormed off to the palace to see the young queen for herself and, on recognizing Snow White, she thought she would die of rage.

But this time there was nothing she could do but put on the magic iron sandals the little men had made and dance until she fell down dead.

And Snow White lived happily ever after.

THE SEVEN
RAVENS
• AND THE SEVEN WOVEN SHIRTS •

There once lived a man and a woman who had seven sons and no daughters. Every day they dreamed of having a baby girl to gladden their days.

Finally, the woman found that she was with child again, and on the day she gave birth, the couple were overjoyed to see that they had a daughter.

The little girl was beautiful, but small and sickly, and they were afraid she might die at any time. So the father sent the seven brothers out with a pitcher to look for water so that they could baptize the little girl.

The seven sons ran to the fountain where they

fought over the pitcher. Each one wanted to be the one to carry the water back for their newborn sister's baptism. In the struggle, the pitcher fell to the ground and shattered. The seven brothers were struck dumb by the sight of the broken pieces of the pitcher scattered around the fountain. They did not dare return home.

Meanwhile, their father was growing impatient. When there was still no sign of his sons after a long while, he exclaimed, "I wish they turned into ravens, every last one!"

And so it was. No sooner were the words out of his mouth than he felt a thrumming in the air, and looking up, saw seven black ravens circling his head. They cawed then disappeared.

The father was despondent and the mother inconsolable, but gradually they found comfort in their beloved daughter, who recovered and grew stronger and more beautiful by the day.

The girl knew nothing of her seven brothers since her parents had made sure she was not told about them. One day in the market, however, she overheard some women whispering together, "Yes, of course, she's quite beautiful, but had it not been for her, her seven brothers would still be here."

The girl ran home to ask her parents what the women meant. When they realized they could no longer keep their secret, they told her what had happened. She listened without saying a word, and could think of nothing but her brothers from that day on.

One night, realizing she would know no peace until she had found her brothers and freed them from the spell, she decided to leave at once and go in search of them. She took one of her mother's rings to remember her by, a chunk of bread for when she was hungry, a small pitcher of water for when she was thirsty and a small chair for when she was tired.

She walked and she walked, farther and farther, until she reached the ends of the earth. There she arrived at the sun's house. She sat down on her little chair to wait, and when the sun appeared, snorting heat and vomiting fire, the girl was very much afraid.

"What is this smell of human flesh so near?" the sun cried. "Who dares approach my house when I'm not here?"

The girl was very much afraid, but she spoke up, "Oh Sun, please help me find my brothers, the seven ravens."

"Help me satisfy my thirst," the sun replied.

The girl offered him the water from her pitcher, but when the sun's rays hit the pitcher, it broke into a thousand pieces.

"Arghh!" the sun cried. "I want human flesh! Human flesh is what I want!

Burning from the heat, the girl ran away before the sun could eat her up.

She walked and she walked until she reached the moon's house, where she sat down on her little chair to wait.

The moon arrived clothed in frost and said in a voice cold as ice, "What is this smell of human flesh so near? Who dares approach my house when I'm not here?"

The girl was very much afraid, but she thought the moon could be no worse than the sun, so she spoke up, "Oh Moon, help me find my brothers, the seven ravens."

"Help me appease my hunger," the moon replied.

The girl offered the bread she carried with her, but when the moon's white beams touched the bread, it turned into stone.

"Ughh!" cried the moon. "I want human flesh! Human flesh is what I want!"

Freezing from the cold, the girl ran away before the moon could eat her up.

She walked and she walked until she reached the house of the stars, where she sat down on her little chair to wait.

The stars arrived, exhausted, and said, "What is this smell of human flesh so near! Who dares approach our house when we're not here?"

The girl was somewhat afraid, but she answered, "I'm looking for my brothers, the seven ravens. Tell me stars, can you help me?"

"We are very tired," the stars said. "Lend us your chair."

The girl gave them her chair, and each star sat down in turn. They all found it quite comfortable. The last to sit down was the morning star, and once it had rested, it said, "Your brothers, the seven ravens, can be found in the crystal mountain. The door to the mountain will only open with this little chicken bone. Take it with you and be careful not to lose it."

"I won't," said the girl.

She wrapped the little chicken bone in a little handkerchief, said goodbye to the stars and continued on her way.

She walked and she walked until she reached the crystal mountain. She took out the little handkerchief to open the door, but when she unfolded it, she saw the chicken bone had disappeared. "What will I do now?" she wailed. "I've lost the present the stars gave me. How will I ever open the door?"

But her resolve to find her brothers was so great that she stopped crying, took out a knife and cut off her baby finger. No sooner had she put it into the keyhole than the door to the crystal mountain opened.

As soon as she entered, a little man approached her. "Little girl, what are you looking for?" he asked.

"I'm looking for my brothers, the seven ravens."

"The ravens aren't home. They should be back soon

though," the little man said and invited her to wait.

The table was set in the dining room — seven plates of food and seven glasses of wine. The girl was very hungry and ate a mouthful from each plate and had a sip from each glass. In the last glass, she dropped her mother's ring. Then she hid behind a curtain.

Just then there was a loud thrumming noise and a cry. "The raven lords are here," the little man announced.

The seven ravens called for food and drink as they entered. When they sat down at the table, they saw someone had eaten from their plates and drunk from their glasses, and they all said together, "A smell of human flesh is in the air! The smell of human flesh lingers here! Who has come to the crystal mountain?"

Six of the ravens searched the dining room, high and low, and when they found the girl hiding behind the curtain, they screeched threateningly, "Who are you? Who are you?"

But the eldest brother was too thirsty to look for the intruder. He had already started drinking his wine. That was when he saw his mother's ring at the bottom of his glass. "Don't screech," he commanded. "Don't threaten her. This is our sister who has come for us," he said.

"Yes, it is me," the girl said. "I've come to break the spell."

"It won't be easy," the little man said. "To break the spell you must weave seven shirts. While you are weaving, you must speak to no one. Only when the seven shirts are finished, and the raven lords have put them on, will the spell be broken. And only then will you be allowed to speak again."

The girl set to work immediately. She sat out in the beautiful garden every day, spinning and spinning and not speaking to anyone, not to the little man nor to the seven ravens circling above.

On one of those days, the king's son passed by the young girl weaving on his way back from hunting. He greeted her and asked what she was doing and who she was. The girl did not say a word. Struck by her beauty, the king's son wanted to take her to the palace and asked if she would go with him. The girl nodded yes, she would. So the prince sent for his carriage and the girl sat inside, still weaving. They set off, followed by the prince's retinue and the little man, while the seven ravens flew behind.

Every day the prince visited the girl in her room and tried to encourage her to speak, but in vain. She just kept weaving. Even though she spent all her time weaving and never spoke, the prince fell in love with her.

Seeing his love for the strange girl, one of the prince's cousins became very jealous. She wanted to marry the prince herself, and she hated the way he spent all day with the girl.

She went to the king and queen and told them that the weaving girl was none other than a witch, toying with the prince, and that she was in league with the little man and that ever since the girl's arrival, seven sinister ravens had been circling the palace night and day.

The king and queen were frightened and ordered a scaffold to be built on which the young girl would be burned alive.

The girl said nothing but just kept weaving, faster and faster. She had already completed six shirts and was working on the last when she was led to the scaffold where a bonfire was being prepared. She kept on weaving as the ravens flew, cawing above. She had only one sleeve left to go, when the flames sprang to life.

Then the little man snatched the seven shirts from her hands and threw them over the seven ravens, who immediately turned into seven elegant young men.

Only the smallest young man, the one wearing the shirt with the missing sleeve, was left with a raven's wing where his arm should have been.

The king, the queen, the prince and all the bystanders could not believe their eyes. The king ordered a halt to the execution and finally the girl spoke, telling her story. The whole assembly was moved by her account, and the king consented to a marriage between his son and the brave young girl.

The ceremony was held the very next day, and the prince and the young girl were very happy.

The seven brothers were appointed as ministers. Those who remember the story say the wisest and most judicious of all was the minister known as Raven's Wing.

THE FROG
PRINCE
• AND THE GOLDEN BALL •

One hot summer's day, the king's youngest daughter went into the woods and sat down by a stream where the water between the rocks formed a quiet pool. The air was cool and shady. The princess had a golden ball with her that she threw into the air and caught as it fell. The golden ball was her favorite toy.

One time, however, she threw the ball so high that instead of falling back into her hands, it fell into the grass, rolled into the pool and disappeared. The king's daughter peered into the water, but the pool was so deep she could not see to the bottom.

"Oh, me!" she wailed. "I've lost my lovely golden ball. What will I do without it? How will I play now?"

As she spoke, she heard a gravelly voice say, "Why are you crying so, Princess?"

When the king's daughter turned to see who was speaking, she saw the head of a fat, ugly frog jutting out of the water.

"What good are you to me, Frog? My little golden ball has fallen into the pool of water, and I won't be able to play with it ever again."

"I can swim to the bottom of the pool and find it for you. But what will you give me if I do?"

"I will give you my dresses and jewelry. I can even give you my golden crown as well."

"I don't want your dresses or your jewelry. I don't want your golden crown, either," the frog said. "I want you to take me to the palace to play with you. I want you to let me sit with you, eat from your little golden plate, drink from your little silver cup, sleep in your soft little bed, and have you treat me kindly. If you promise to do all that for me, then I will bring you your golden ball."

The frog's words sounded like nonsense to the princess, since frogs could not live out of water. And so she said, "I promise. Bring me my lovely golden ball."

The frog dove into the deep pool and resurfaced a minute later holding the golden ball in his mouth. He swam to shore and dropped the ball onto the grass.

As soon as she saw her golden ball, the princess ran to pick it up. She was so happy to have it back that she completely forgot about the frog and rushed back to the palace.

"Croak! Croak!" called the frog. "Take me with you as you promised."

But the princess didn't stop until she reached the palace. She didn't even hear the frog calling.

The next day when the princess, the king and all the courtiers were sitting down for their meal, a strange noise was heard — splish, splash, splish, splash — as though a heavy, wet object was climbing the marble staircase. Then came the sound of a soft knock on the door and the words:

> OPEN THE DOOR,
> O PRINCESS, YOUNG THING.
> REMEMBER YOUR PROMISE
> MADE DOWN BY THE SPRING.

The princess ran to open the door, thinking she recognized the gravelly voice calling her. Behind the door was the frog that she had so completely forgotten. Frightened half to death, she slammed the door shut and returned to her place at the table.

But the king could hear her heart pounding, and he asked, "What are you afraid of, dear daughter?"

"The frog from the pool, Father."

"What does the frog want with you?"

"When I was playing by the stream yesterday, my golden ball rolled into the pool, and I couldn't get it out. The frog went after it for me, and I promised to take him to the palace. In truth, I didn't think he was capable of leaving the water and coming this far."

Just then, there was another soft knock at the door, and the frog said:

> OPEN THE DOOR,
>
> O PRINCESS, YOUNG THING.
>
> REMEMBER YOUR PROMISE
>
> MADE DOWN BY THE SPRING.

Then the king said, "A king's daughter always keeps her promises. Go and open the door."

The princess stood up from the table, walked over to the door and opened it. The frog hopped inside and followed her to her seat — splish, splash, splish, splash. The princess sat down and tried to resume eating as though nothing had happened. But the frog said, "Put me on your chair so we can sit together."

The princess hesitated, but the king ordered her to do as she had been told. She picked up the frog with two fingers and put him beside her. Next, the frog wanted to be put on the table. The king glared at her and, once again, she picked up the frog with two fingers and set him on the table.

The frog said, "Push your little golden plate closer to me so we can both eat."

The princess did as she was told, and the frog ate a hearty meal. She, however, was unable to take so much as a bite.

"I've had enough to eat," the frog said, "and now

I'm tired. Take me upstairs to your bedroom and put me in your soft, silky bed."

The princess began to cry since she did not want to have to touch the frog again, not to mention having to sleep with him in her soft, clean little bed. But the king ordered her to obey. "Never look down on those who helped you when you were in need," he said.

Still sobbing, the princess picked up the frog, carried him to her room and put him on the small embroidered pillow where he slept the night away.

The next morning, the frog woke up and — splish, splash, splish, splash — hopped down the stairs and out into the woods.

"Thank goodness!" said the princess. "He's gone and won't bother me again."

But she was wrong.

That night she heard the heavy wet hopping sound again — splish, splash, splish, splash — and had to take the frog to the table, feed him and take him to her room. The exact same thing happened on the third night, except this time the frog asked her to give him a kiss. The princess immediately refused, but the frog said, "If you don't, I'll tell your father."

So with great disgust, the princess did as the frog asked. But then she picked him up and threw him against the wall. "That will shut you up, frog," she said.

No sooner had the frog hit the wall and fallen to the ground than he turned into a handsome young prince with gentle eyes.

"A wicked witch cast a spell on me," the prince told her. "I was to remain a frog until a princess agreed to take me from the pool and sleep with me for three nights in a row. You have broken the spell. Nothing would make me happier than if you would agree to be my wife."

The princess was still reeling with surprise, but she had all night to think this over. She watched the prince, sleeping peacefully, now free of the spell that had bound him. The next morning, when a splendid coach drew up pulled by eight white horses, she knew she wanted to leave with him.

Even the king welcomed the marriage.

The prince and princess lived together for many happy years, so many that the princess forgot about her lovely golden ball and all the fun she used to have playing with it.

THE THREE FEATHERS
• OR THE FROG PRINCESS •

Many, many years ago there lived a king who had three sons. The two eldest sons were quick-witted and comely, but the youngest son spoke little, was simple and forever scatterbrained. The older brothers nicknamed him John the Fool.

The old king, knowing he would soon die, wanted to leave his kingdom to the son best suited to govern it. But he was not sure which son that should be.

Finally, one day, he called his three sons to him and said, "Go out into the world all three of you. He who brings back the finest carpet will be king when I am gone."

The sons thought this a strange request, but they prepared for their departure. On the morning they were to leave, the king accompanied them into the garden and blew three feathers into the air.

"Each of you will follow the direction shown by one of the feathers," he said.

One feather blew to the East. That was the direction the oldest brother took. Another feather blew to the West. That was the direction the middle brother took. But the third feather blew a short distance straight ahead and fell to the ground. The other brothers made fun of John the Fool who would now have to stay put.

Feeling sad, John the Fool sat on the ground where his feather had fallen. Then he noticed a little trap-door that he had never seen before. He lifted it up, saw a staircase and followed it down. At the end of the staircase was another door. John knocked three times and heard a voice inside say:

WHO IS THAT KNOCKING AT THE DOOR?
WHAT CAN HE POSSIBLY WANT ME FOR?

The door opened. Inside, John the Fool saw a green frog sitting on a stone throne next to the crystal clear waters of a pond.

"What are you looking for?" the frog asked.

"I'm looking for the finest carpet in the world."

"You shall have it," the frog said, handing him a walnut. "Open this when the time is right."

John the Fool was happy to take the walnut and return to the palace.

•

The two brothers were away for several days. "John the Fool won't find anything worthwhile, being the fool he is," they thought to themselves. So they did not go to too much trouble looking for the finest carpet.

When they reported back to the king, the two brothers held out the carpets they had found. The king examined them, felt their coarse weave and said to John, "What did you bring me?"

John took the walnut from his pocket, and his two brothers started to laugh.

"John has brought a walnut. What a fool!"

"Could this walnut be what you have brought to show me?" asked the king gravely.

Remembering the frog's words, John opened the walnut and a splendid carpet with a fine, delicate weave fell out.

They were all dumbstruck.

The king announced that his kingdom would be John's, since he had clearly brought back the most beautiful carpet.

But the older brothers insisted on another test.

"Father," they said to the king. "John is incapable of governing, he doesn't have the wits for it."

The king let himself be convinced and agreed to a new test. The kingdom would go to the brother who could bring back the most beautiful ring.

He went with his three sons into the garden and blew the three feathers into the air. The first blew to the East. That was the direction the oldest brother took. The second feather blew to the West. That was the direction the middle brother took. The third feather blew to the ground and fell not far from where they stood, next to the trapdoor, just as it had the first time.

John the Fool lifted up the trapdoor, followed the stairs down, knocked on the door and heard the same voice as before:

WHO IS THAT KNOCKING AT THE DOOR?
WHAT CAN HE POSSIBLY WANT ME FOR?

The door opened and there was the green frog sitting on her stone throne. "What have you come for now?" she asked.

"My father has asked us to bring him the most beautiful ring," John answered.

"You shall have it," the frog said, and she held out another walnut. "Open it when the time is right."

John was happy as he returned to the palace.

It took several days for his brothers to return. They had not bothered looking too hard. They bought a few copper rings in the first town they passed through.

When the king heard his three sons were back, he called them to him. "Show me your rings," he said.

The older brothers pulled out the rings they had bought. The king examined them, then asked, "What about the ring you brought back for me, John?"

John reached into his pocket and brought out the walnut. His brothers started to laugh.

"A walnut! Father, he's brought another walnut!"

John opened the nut to reveal the most beautiful ring inside, delicately crafted and adorned with sparkling precious stones.

The king was greatly impressed and said, "John, the kingdom is yours. You have clearly brought back the most beautiful ring."

Once again the brothers objected, telling their father that John would never know how to govern, not having the wits required.

Once again, their father let himself be convinced. He said, "Since the three of you must be wed, the time has come to look for a wife. The kingdom will go to the man who brings back the most beautiful fiancée."

Once again he blew the feathers into the air, and the sons followed their directions.

John's feather flew to the ground and settled next to the trapdoor. John opened the trapdoor, followed the stairs down and knocked. The same voice said:

WHO IS THAT KNOCKING AT THE DOOR?
WHAT CAN HE POSSIBLY WANT ME FOR?

"What have you come for this time?" the frog asked.

"My father has told us to come back with the most beautiful fiancée."

"I could be your fiancée," said the frog. "Would you marry me, John?"

The question took John by surprise. Although he would not call the frog beautiful — far from it — she had certainly been good to him, so he answered, "Yes, I will marry you."

"Good," the frog said. "I will hop into the walnut, and you open it when the time is right." And so she did.

John went back to the palace and had to wait two weeks for his brothers' return.

His brothers found two sturdy peasant girls in two

distant towns, and came home feeling pleased with themselves. "John the Fool will never be able to find a beautiful fiancée. Never!" they thought.

The father called all three to him and asked them to introduce their fiancées. The older brothers brought forward the two peasant girls for the king to see. The king glanced at them, then looked up. "What about you, John?" he asked. "Where is your fiancée?"

John pulled the walnut from his pocket.

"The walnut again!" his brothers laughed.

John decided the time had come to open the walnut — not without some misgivings, however, since the frog would pale beside his brothers' fiancées. But he had given his word to marry her and could not go back on it. So he shut his eyes and opened the walnut.

Instead of the frog John expected, a lovely woman stepped out wearing an elegant green gown as transparent as water.

"This is without a doubt the most beautiful woman," their father decreed. "John will be my heir."

Once again, the brothers complained angrily and begged the king to reconsider, "We cannot agree to making John the Fool king," they said.

The king decided he would put the matter to rest with one last test. He hung a golden hoop in the middle of the hall. "All three young women must try to jump through the hoop," he said.

The brothers' fiancées were heavy and clumsy, and both fell on their first attempts. But John the Fool's fiancée jumped through the hoop without touching it, as light and agile as a frog.

The brothers could say nothing more. John was crowned king and governed wisely for many years.

As for the queen, she enjoyed playing with the golden hoop for many a year to come.

BEARSKIN

• AND THE LOYAL FIANCÉE •

Once upon a time there was a young man who enlisted as a soldier and fought valiantly in every battle. When peace was declared, his captain told him he was free to go where he pleased.

The soldier returned to his parents' home, but his parents had died and his brothers, all married by now, had become accustomed to living without him and did not want to have him in their homes.

"What will we do with you?" they said. "We don't need you for anything. It's best that you make your own way in the world."

The soldier shouldered his musket, his only possession, and went out into the bleak, oh so bleak, world. He reached a meadow with a circle of trees in the middle of it, and sat under one of the trees to ponder his fate. "I have no money," he thought. "All I know how to do is to wage war. Now that peace has been declared, I'll die of starvation."

No sooner had that thought crossed his mind than he heard a low hum behind him, and turning around, he saw an elegant gentleman wearing a long, green dresscoat. Peeking out from underneath the dresscoat, however, was an ugly tail and a frightening cloven hoof.

"I know what you need," said the gentleman, having read the soldier's thoughts. "I can give you all the money in the world, but you must show me how brave you are."

"That's easy," replied the soldier, keeping his voice

from trembling, although he already suspected who was speaking to him. "Put me to the test."

"Fine," the man said. "Look behind you."

The soldier turned to see a huge growling bear charging straight at him.

"How about a little tickle for your muzzle, you big brute," he said laughing, then took aim with his musket. He fired and the bear fell dead at his feet.

"I see you are not lacking in courage," the man in the green dresscoat said. "As I promised, you will have all the money your heart desires, on one condition."

"So long as the condition doesn't affect the salvation of my soul," the soldier said, since he already knew that the gentleman in the green dresscoat was none other than the devil himself.

"That depends on you," the gentleman said. "You cannot bathe for seven years, nor trim your beard, nor your hair, nor your fingernails, nor say the Our Father. I will give you my dresscoat and an overcoat that you must wear throughout those seven years. If you die within that time, you will belong to me. But if you remain alive, you will be free and wealthy for the rest of your days."

The soldier considered his great need and how often he had stared down death successfully, and he decided to run the risk one more time. He agreed.

The devil took off his green dresscoat, gave it to the soldier and said, "Every time you reach into the coat pocket you will pull out a handful of gold."

Then he removed the bear's skin and said, "This will be the overcoat that you must wear at all times. Because of it, you will be called Bearskin."

At that, the devil disappeared.

The soldier pulled on the dresscoat, put his hand in the pocket, and saw that it was true — he brought out a handful of gold coins. Feeling very happy, he threw the bearskin over his shoulders and struck off, prepared to make the best of his lot.

●

That first year, his vow to the devil did not weigh too heavily on him, but by the second year he had begun to look like a monster. His hair cascaded over his shoulders in matted strands, his beard reached down to his chest, he had claws on the ends of his fingers and his whole body was grimy and stank. Whoever crossed his path quickly ran away. But since he gave money to the poor, wherever he went, and asked them to pray for him, and since he paid well, he was always able to find a place to stay.

In the fourth year, he stopped at an inn, but the innkeeper did not want to let him stay, not even in the stable, since he was afraid his horses would take fright. But when Bearskin reached into his pocket

three times in a row and brought out a handful of gold coins each time, the innkeeper relented. He gave him a room in a building in the back, but asked him not to show his face so that the inn would not get a bad reputation.

Bearskin stayed there for several weeks.

One afternoon as he sat alone wishing with all his heart that the seven years would soon be over, he heard loud wailing in the room next door. Since he was a compassionate man, he opened the door and discovered an old man holding his head in his hands and crying in anguish.

Bearskin approached the man to comfort him, but at the sight of Bearskin, the man took fright and tried to flee. He only calmed down when Bearskin spoke, realizing that the frightful apparition had a human voice. Bearskin convinced the old man to tell him why he was in such despair. The old man confessed he was ruined, that he had lost his estate and was so poor, he could not even pay for his room at the inn.

"Well, if that's your only worry," Bearskin said, "I have money enough to help you." He paid for the old man's room, and gave him a sack full of money so that he could cancel his debts.

The man was overcome with gratitude and did not know how to thank Bearskin enough. "Come with me," he said. "I have three beautiful daughters. You may choose one of them as your wife. When I tell them what you have done for me, not one of them will refuse you. The truth is, you do look rather strange, but it won't matter to them."

Bearskin liked the idea and agreed to accompany him. But when the eldest daughter saw him, she was so frightened she started to scream and ran away. The second daughter said nothing at first, but just looked him up and down. Then she said, "How can I accept a man who doesn't even look human? I would rather marry the circus bear we saw last summer. At least they shaved him and clothed him in a hussar's jacket and white gloves."

However, the youngest daughter said to her father, "This must be a good man to have helped you, and if you have promised him a wife, you must keep your promise. I will marry him."

Bearskin's face was so covered in grit and grime, no one could see how happy he was at her words. He took a ring off his finger, broke it in two and gave the young girl one half. He kept the other half for himself and said, "We cannot marry yet. I must keep traveling for three more years. Take good care of this half of the ring, and if I have not returned at the end of three years, you will be free, since that will mean I have died. But please, pray to God every day to keep me alive."

Bearskin left and his fiancée dressed all in black. Tears sprang to her eyes whenever she thought about him. "Who is this strange, generous man?" she wondered. But her older sisters made fun of her.

"Be careful, bears like sweets and if he likes you, he'll eat you up...I wonder what a bear's caress is like... This should be a fun wedding, bears being such good dancers and all!"

Their sister said nothing.

•

Meanwhile, Bearskin traveled to the ends of the earth and back, handing out money and food to the poor so that they would pray for him.

Finally, when he could not stand the awful bearskin and the dreadful filth any longer, the last days of the seven years were upon him. He returned to the meadow where he had found the circle of trees and sat down to wait for the devil. Soon after, the wind picked up and the devil appeared. Furiously, he threw the old soldier's jacket and two bags of gold at Bearskin, then demanded he return his green dresscoat.

Bearskin gladly handed over the dresscoat and the devil disappeared.

Bearskin jumped into the river straightaway, bathed, cut his hair, shaved off his beard and burned the bear's skin he had worn for seven years.

He made his way into town, bought himself a fine velvet jacket and a carriage drawn by four white horses, and set off for his fiancée's house.

No one recognized him. His fiancée's father thought he was a gentleman of some importance and led him to the room where his daughters were to be found. He sat down between the two eldest daughters who offered him wine and sweets. They thought they had never seen a more elegant man in their lives. His fiancée, dressed all in black, sat across from him and did not open her mouth or look up once.

Then the gentleman asked the father if he would be willing to give him one of his daughters in marriage. The two eldest daughters leapt from their seats and rushed to their rooms to dress in their finest, each one thinking she would be the lucky one.

As soon as he was left alone with the youngest daughter, the stranger pulled out the half of the ring he had kept, dropped it into a glass of wine and offered the glass to her. She took a few sips then heard something clink in the bottom of the glass. She peered inside. Seeing the other half of the ring, her heart began to pound. She took the half she wore on a chain around her neck, fished the other half from the glass, joined them together and saw that they were a perfect match.

"I'm your fiancé," the stranger said, "the one you

know as Bearskin. By the grace of God, I have regained my human form."

He crossed the room, took her in his arms and kissed her. Just then the two sisters walked in. When they saw that the handsome young man had chosen their younger sister, and that he was none other than Bearskin, they stomped off furiously.

But their fury mattered little to the fiancés, who were married the next day and lived happily ever after.

NOTES

The versions of the fairy tales in this Little Book are based on the collection NURSERY AND HOUSEHOLD TALES, which the brothers Jakob and Wilhelm Grimm recorded in Germany, early in the nineteenth century, and on TALES OF LONG AGO WITH MORALS, published by Charles Perrault in Paris, in the late seventeenth century. Other references consulted were the works of folklore researchers A.R. Almodóvar in Spain, Iona and Peter Opie in England and Jack Zipes' book, THE GREAT FAIRY TALE TRADITION: FROM STRAPAROLA AND BASILE TO THE BROTHERS GRIMM.

Bruno Bettelheim's insightful observations in his book, THE USES OF ENCHANTMENT: THE MEANING AND IMPORTANCE OF FAIRY TALES, were taken into consideration in choosing the stories. His views also guided the emphasis placed here on certain passages and the decision to include elements, which in his judgment, are important for children's emotional growth.

A few notes about each of the versions follow.

Puss-in-Boots

Stories in which a small, seemingly unimportant animal is transformed into a wonderful, ingenious helper are common in the oral tradition of many countries. But it is rare for a cat to be the animal whose ingeniousness brings good fortune to his unfortunate master. Nevertheless, that is precisely what occurs in "Puss-in-Boots," which has become one of the most popular children's stories.

The first printed version of this picaresque tale is found in Giovan Francesco Straparola's LE PIACEVOLI NOTTI (Pleasant Nights) published in Italy in 1550. The story is entitled "Constantino Fortunato" and begins with the death of a poor woman who leaves her children a kneading trough, a pastry board and a cat. The cat is inherited by the youngest son.

Between 1634 and 1636, Giambattista Basile published the five volumes of LO CUNTO DE LI CUNTI OVERO LO TRATTENEMIENTO DE PECCERILLE (commonly known as IL PENTAMERONE or THE TALE OF TALES in English), a collection of fabulous stories from the oral tradition, including "Cagliuso." In this tale, a beggar's youngest son also receives what seems to be the worst part of an inheritance — a cat.

Sixty years later, Charles Perrault published TALES OF LONG AGO and included a tale with the same motif entitled "Puss-in-Boots." Curiously enough, in the two oldest versions by Straparola and Basile, the clever animal is a female, not a male cat.

The Brothers Grimm included "Puss-in-Boots" in the first edition of KINDER-UND-HAUSMÄRCHEN (1812), but since it closely resembled Perrault's tale, it was omitted in subsequent editions.

Bruno Bettelheim considers "Puss-in-Boots" to belong to a group of picaresque stories, which are as widespread in the oral tradition as fairy tales. He points out that their importance for children lies in acknowledging that apparently insignificant characters — which is the way children sometimes see themselves — can be responsible for extraordinary achievements, like the cat in the tale who, through his ingeniousness, finds a way to swallow an ogre.

The version in this Little Book is based on Charles Perrault's tale.

LITTLE RED RIDING HOOD

This is another of the most popular traditional tales, although the source used by Charles Perrault has not been clearly established. Perrault published the first written version of this tale in 1697 in TALES OF LONG AGO.

Jack Zipes claims in his book THE GREAT FAIRY TALE TRADITION that "Little Red Riding Hood" may have been part of a story cycle related to initiation rites in seamstress communities in the south of France. He mentions one tale entitled "The Grandmother" in which a young peasant girl must take bread and milk to her grandmother who lives in the woods. At a crossroads, she meets up with the wolf who asks her which path she will take — pins or needles. She chooses the needles path. The wolf reaches the grandmother's house first, eats her and then slips into her bed to wait for his next victim.

The versions we know today come from the Brothers Grimm ("Rotkäppchen") and Charles Perrault ("Le petit chaperon rouge"). Both have similar beginnings and developments, however there is a marked difference in the dénouements.

Perrault's version ends when the wolf eats Little Red Riding Hood. It is followed by a moral in verse warning little girls not to be taken in by the many wolves that abound in the world: "...Young children, as we clearly see,/Pretty girls, especially,/Innocent of all life's dangers,/Shouldn't stop and chat with strangers..."

On the other hand, the Brothers Grimm save Little Red

Riding Hood. A hunter approaches on hearing the snoring of the wolf, who has eaten the grandmother and Little Red Riding Hood. Guessing what has happened, the hunter slits opens the wolf's belly, and Little Red Riding Hood and her grandmother jump out. Afterward, the three of them place a rock in the wolf's belly, and the wolf dies. This is followed by an epilogue in which Little Red Riding Hood must go to her grandmother's house again, but this time she does not dawdle along the way, and she ignores another wolf who tries to approach her. She arrives at her grandmother's house, and together they trick the second big bad wolf into falling into a pot of boiling water where he drowns.

According to Bettelheim, the Brothers Grimm's version with its happy ending is much more popular than Perrault's tale and moral, because the former better reflects young children's concern with leaving the parental home and going out into the world. The Brothers Grimm's version is a metaphorical allusion to the dangers that lurk when one abandons the protected haven of home and must make one's decisions independently. The end shows that despite having made mistakes, one can emerge successfully and freely.

Perrault's tale, on the other hand, explicitly states that what happens is an act of seduction. After devouring the grandmother, the wolf does not don her clothes. He simply gets into her bed, and when Little Red Riding Hood arrives, he invites her to lie down with him. "Little Red Riding Hood got undressed and climbed into bed, where she was most surprised to see what her grandmother was like with nothing on." Then comes the famous series of statements ("What big eyes you have!..."). The version of "Little Red Riding Hood" in this book is based on the Brothers Grimm's tale with the addition of some of Perrault's twists and apt descriptions.

SLEEPING BEAUTY

Both the Brothers Grimm and Perrault include this story in their books. Charles Perrault's is entitled "La belle au bois dormant" and is the longest of the prose texts in his slim collection. In the Brothers Grimm's edition, the story is called "Dornröschen."

One of the oldest versions of "Sleeping Beauty" appears in LO CUNTO DE LI CUNTI by Giambattista Basile. In this tale, "Sun, Moon and Talia," a powerful king calls together the wise men of his court to prophesy his newborn daughter Talia's future. The wise men tell him the child will be in great danger when, as a young girl, a thread of flax pricks her beneath her fingernail. The king responds by prohibiting all of his subjects from spinning flax, hemp or any similar material. However, many years later, Talia meets an old woman spinning. Since she has never seen a spinning wheel before, she is very curious about the unknown artifact. She takes the spindle herself and begins spinning the flax. No sooner has she begun, than a thread pricks her beneath her fingernail and she falls down dead. Overcome with sorrow, the king places her lifeless body on a velvet chair and abandons the castle. Time passes until one day, a prince out hunting in the vicinity loses his falcon. The falcon flies through one of the castle windows and does not return. The prince enters the castle looking for the falcon, finds Talia, falls in love with the sleeping girl and returns to visit her often. Nine months later, two baby boys are born. The fairies look after them and put them at their sleeping mother's breast to nurse. One day, one of the babies mistakes Talia's finger for his mother's breast and begins to suckle. The thread falls out and Talia awakens.

There are several differences between the two versions of "Sleeping Beauty" by Perrault and the Brothers Grimm:
• The Brothers Grimm end the tale with a kiss from the prince that awakens the beautiful princess who has been sleeping for one hundred years. Perrault adds a second part that

includes a crude episode of cannibalism similar to the one in the Basile version.

• In Perrault's tale, the invitation goes out to seven fairies. In the Grimm's tale, only twelve fairies are invited since the royal couple has only twelve golden plates.

• In Perrault's story, each of the seven fairies is given "a thick gold casket containing a knife, fork, and spoon of fine gold, decorated with diamonds and rubies." Not only do the king and queen forget to invite the oldest fairy in the kingdom, they also do not have a casket for her.

• In the Grimm's version, the entire court falls asleep, not just the princess. In Perrault's tale, when the princess falls asleep, the good fairy returns to the castle and decides it is best for the princess to wake up surrounded by her court and servants. So, with her magic wand, she puts them to sleep one after the other, except for the king and queen who abandon the castle.

Bettelheim points out that the tale is a reflection of the long period of passivity and lethargy that often accompanies the beginning of adolescence. Adolescents need to focus on themselves, and recognize and gather their strength, so that they can go out into the world with energy and determination. He also points out that the tale is full of

Freudian symbols such as the spindle, the narrow winding staircase, the room hidden in a tower and the small key with which the door is opened.

This version of "Sleeping Beauty" is based on the Grimm's plot, but includes some of the developments, descriptions, details and humorous dialogue from Perrault's tale. For instance, when the princess wakes up one hundred years later to the prince's kiss, she stretches her limbs and says, "What took you so long, my prince?"

CINDERELLA

The origins of "Cinderella" are remote. Some researchers suggest that the theme of a young girl neglected by her father and mistreated by her stepmother and stepsisters has been part of oral literature since the fifth century. Others link this story to a Chinese tale from the ninth century, and point out that the symbol of a slipper so small it could only fit the most beautiful maiden harkens back to one of the attributes of feminine beauty in ancient China, namely tiny feet.

"La gatta Cenerentola," which is included in LO CUNTI DE LI CUNTI by Giambattista Basile, seems to be the first published version. In it we find all the characteristic motifs of this tale: the widowed father who takes on a new wife, the daughter who is evicted from her place in the paternal home and relegated to the hearth and the ashes (or cinders), the ball in the prince's castle, the magical transformation of rags into gorgeous finery, the little slipper lost on the staircase, the recognition of its true owner, and the restitution of the neglected daughter to her rightful place.

Both the Brothers Grimm and Perrault include versions of "Cinderella" in their collections, respectively entitled "Aschenputtel" and "Cendrillon." Currently, Perrault's is the better-known version — his tale is shorter, more structured and more literary than the Grimm's. The oral and folk origins of the story are still visible in the Brothers Grimm's version, although the authors did polish the language and clean up the racier passages of the tales they collected in the former county of Hanau, Germany, in the early nineteenth century.

The plot in the two versions of "Cinderella" — Perrault's and the Brothers Grimm's — differs in a few major ways:

• The Brothers Grimm's tale begins with the death of Cinderella's mother. Just before she dies, she calls Cinderella to her and tells her not to be sad because she will always protect her. Perrault's tale, on the other hand, begins with the father as a widower who remarries.

• The fairy godmother only appears in Perrault's version. The presents come from her — the dress and glass slippers, the carriage, horses, coachman and footmen — during the unforgettable scene in which she uses her magic wand to turn mice and a pumpkin into beautiful horses and a coach. In the Grimm's version, a white bird nesting in a tree by Cinderella's mother's grave bestows the presents of which there are only two — a dress and golden slippers.

• In Perrault's tale, the action develops along simpler lines. There are only two balls from which Cinderella flees, and she loses her slipper at the second one. In the Grimm's version, Cinderella attends three balls and her flight is complicated and difficult. First she climbs into a dovecot, then into a pear tree, and fleeing from the last ball, she leaves her slipper behind.

• In the Brothers Grimm's version, when Cinderella asks to go to the ball, her godmother imposes one condition — that Cinderella pick out the lentils from the ashes, a seemingly impossible task, but one that Cinderella manages with the help of her dear friends, the birds. In Perrault's tale, there is no such episode.

• The dénouement is not the same in the two versions. In the Grimm's tale, the two stepsisters are punished for their wickedness — Cinderella's friends, the doves, peck their eyes, blinding them. The dénouement is the exact opposite in Perrault's tale, not vengeful at all, but courteous. Cinderella forgives her stepsisters and marries them to two lords of the court.

Certain details also distinguish one version from the other:

• In Grimm, the slipper is made of gold; in Perrault, of glass.
• In Grimm, the prince puts tar on the staircase making the gold slipper stick, while in Perrault, Cinderella's slipper simply falls off.
• In Grimm, when the stepsisters try on the little slipper and realize it does not fit, one cuts off her toes, the other her heel. In Perrault, this bloody scene is omitted.

Perrault's tale is more refined, and perhaps for that very reason, more popular. The Grimm's version is longer and more complex, yet both have lovely, significant episodes. That explains why this version, although based on Perrault, incorporates some of the lovely touches from the Grimm's tale while omitting some of Perrault's courtly asides.

According to Bruno Bettelheim, "Cinderella" is a fairy tale that reflects as few others do the intimate experiences of a child suffering from sibling rivalry. Cinderella is subject to abuse from her stepsisters, she is made to carry out demeaning chores for which she is never given a word of thanks and, instead, is asked to make even greater sacrifices. She must constantly look after her stepsisters' needs, forgetting her own. "Exaggerated though Cinderella's tribulations and degradation may seem to the adult, the child carried away by sibling rivalry feels, 'That's me; that's how they mistreat me, or would want to; that's how little they think of me.' And there are moments — often long time periods — when for inner reasons a child feels this way even when his position among his siblings may seem to give him no cause for it."

Cinderella's final triumph over her stepsisters is comforting for children. It allows them to harbor the hope that even if "relegated to the cinders," their true worth will be recognized.

RUMPELSTILTSKIN

Folklorists have found many versions of this fairy tale throughout Europe, from Scandinavia to Italy and Spain. It is a strange tale that includes several motifs common to fairy tales: the spindle and spinning wheel and the challenge of spinning straw into gold; a defenseless young girl at a loss to know what to do in a dilemma; the appearance of a helper, a bizarre imp who saves her life by carrying out the impossible task of spinning straw into gold himself. But the same strange being who shows such generosity and compassion holds her to the worst vow of all — having to give up her firstborn. This is the same vow the witch has Rapunzel's parents make.

It is interesting to note that the power of certain characters such as this imp, as well as witches and wizards, often lies in their secret name. Once the name is discovered, their power disappears. The scenes in which the queen tries to guess the imp's name are, in fact, the most appealing, and perhaps for that reason, the tale is known by the name of the bizarre character who is equally ready to help and torment the young girl.

In the various regions where the tale is part of the oral tradition, the character's name changes: Ricdin-Ricdon in France, Tom Tit Tot or Trit-a-trot in different parts of England, Whoopity Stoorie in Scotland, and Titeliture, Panzimanzi or Batzibitzili in other parts of Europe. But the name most widely used today, and the name used by the Brothers Grimm in their collection, is Rumpelstiltskin.

The version in this Little Book is based on the story published in the Brothers Grimm's Nursery and Household Tales.

RAPUNZEL

The motif of a damsel imprisoned in a tower appears in the Greek myth of Danaë, the daughter of the King of Argos, who is imprisoned in a bronze tower to protect her from the passion her beauty inspires. But even there she is visited by Zeus who, appearing in the shape of golden rain, impregnates Danaë, and they have a child, Perseus. Many tales pick up on this motif and on the prohibition against cutting one's hair. Seclusion during puberty is a purification and protection rite for young girls in many cultures, and the "Rapunzel" story reflects this ancient custom. Nevertheless, fairy tales show that a parent's desire to isolate and protect a daughter is doomed to fail, and that her seclusion usually ends with her rescue by a prince who then marries her.

Another recurring motif in folktales is that of the pregnant woman who has an uncontrollable craving for special foods, either a fruit or a vegetable. According to popular belief, her cravings must be satisfied. If they are not, her child may be born with a defect. Giambattista Basile tells the story of "Petrosinella," in which a woman expecting her first child desperately wants some parsley from an ogress's garden. Instead of parsley, the Brothers Grimm's version uses rampion, a type of turnip called rapunzel in German. In other words, in both cases the heroine of the tale bears the name of the food her mother craved during her pregnancy.

According to Bettelheim, fantasy, escape, recovery and comfort are all found in "Rapunzel," which is why it is a particularly important tale for small children. It tells them that we have, in our own bodies, the means of obtaining what we desire. Rapunzel's strong, long braids enable the prince to join her in the tower. Also, at the end of the story, Rapunzel's tears restore the prince's sight after he has been blinded by thorns.

This version is based on the Brothers Grimm's tale. For purely aesthetic reasons, the German name Rapunzel has been kept since the proper name Rapónchigo, which appears in some Spanish versions, seemed unattractive for a beautiful young maiden.

THE PEASANT'S CLEVER DAUGHTER

Stories of riddles or puzzles and ingenious ways of solving them are popular worldwide, especially among storytellers because of the immediate interest they arouse in an audience.

One of the most well-known and widely circulated stories is "The Peasant's Clever Daughter." Although there are many variants of this tale, all agree that a king hears about a young, very clever girl, has her brought to the palace and puts her to the test. The young girl always shows herself to be more cunning and clever than the king who, thoroughly taken with her intelligence, decides to marry her. The tests to which the king puts the girl are varied but, generally speaking, he presents her with a number of paradoxical challenges. For instance, he demands that she turn up at court clothed and naked, at night and day, on foot and on a donkey. There are other versions in which the king asks questions that the young girl answers with ready wit.

According to the folklorist Stith Thompson, one of the oldest stories about clever characters is "The Emperor and the Abbott" from the twelfth century. The plot is very simple. The emperor announces to the abbott that if within a given time frame he is not able to answer three questions, he will be sentenced to death. The abbott despairs, but he comes across a miller who tells him he is capable of solving any riddle or answering any question. So the miller disguises himself as the abbott and appears before the emperor. The emperor asks, "How far away is heaven?"

"A day's journey," the miller answers.

"How so?"

"Because it took Jesus one day to get there."

"How much am I worth?"

"Twenty-nine pieces of silver."

"How so?"

"Because they sold Jesus for thirty and you must be worth a least one piece of silver less."

"What am I thinking?"

"You think I am the abbott."

The protagonist's cleverness is what makes these tales so appealing. Each storyteller comes up with new questions and answers. Folklorists have found as many as six hundred variants of this same story.

The version published here is based on the Brothers Grimm's tale.

Snow White

This, too, is another of the most well-known fairy tales, which was popularized by the animated film made by Walt Disney in 1938, his first feature film.

The version known today is the one collected by the Brothers Grimm in Kassel, in the early nineteenth century, entitled "Sneewittchen" although, according to folklorists, many versions of this story can be found throughout Europe, Asia Minor and Africa.

An earlier story with very similar themes appears in Il Pentamerone with the title "The Young Slave." It is the story of Lisa, a beautiful girl, who, it seems, dies when she pricks herself with a poisoned comb. She is placed inside a glass coffin where she not only continues to look fresh and lovely, but also continues to grow. What's more, the coffin grows with her! The story also has a mother figure who is jealous of the girl's beauty, just like the stepmother in the Grimm's fairy tale.

According to Bettelheim, this is a tale that reveals deep oedipal conflicts and clearly shows the stages of child development: a conflictless childhood; puberty, when competition with and jealousy of the mother surface (in this tale, the mother is disguised as the stepmother); a stage of growing maturity and acceptance of responsibilities (in the little men's home, Snow White must work in order to stay); passivity and introversion; inner growth (Snow White asleep in the glass coffin); and, finally, sexual awakening (the prince's kiss saves her from seeming death).

The version given here is based on the Brothers Grimm's tale minus one crude and violent passage. When the stepmother orders Snow White to be killed, she asks that the young girl's liver and lungs be brought back to her as proof. The hunter brings back the viscera of a young boar after which "The cook had to salt them, and the wicked Queen ate them, and thought she had eaten the lung and liver of Snow-white."

This cannibalistic passage does not appear in the first edition of the Grimm's tales, but was incorporated in the second and subsequent editions. According to Maria Tatar, in later editions of NURSERY AND HOUSEHOLD TALES, Wilhelm Grimm dedicated himself to purging all episodes of a sexual nature — insinuations of incest or premarital relations — while emphasizing passages and descriptions of great violence.

THE SEVEN RAVENS

Stith Thompson describes this as a "loyal sister" tale, of which there are many variants. They all have the same central motif, however. Brothers — either seven or twelve of them — are turned into ravens (or swans or doves) at the birth of their baby sister, and abandon the parental home. Years later, when the sister learns of her brothers' existence and of the spell that keeps them far from home, she sets out to find them. She must walk to the ends of the earth and beyond and accomplish many arduous tasks before freeing her brothers. In some versions, she must visit the houses of the sun, the moon, the stars and finally, the crystal mountain.

Sometimes the tale ends when the sister reaches the crystal mountain. The very act of completing the journey is enough of a sacrifice to break the spell over her brothers. In other tales, she must weave seven shirts for each of the ravens. In still others, she must remain mute until she has completed her task.

Giambattista Basile tells a similar story in "I sette colombelli" ("The Seven Doves"), in which the sister must walk to the house of the Mother of Time in order to break the spell on her brothers.

This book follows the Brothers Grimm's version, with the inclusion from other variants of the obligation to weave the seven shirts and the vow of silence needed to break the spell. The final episode in which the youngest brother is left with one raven wing instead of an arm comes from "The Six Swans," another tale from the Brothers Grimm.

The Frog Prince

This is one of many stories in which a young man or woman has a spell cast on him or her by an evil witch or a wicked gnome, and has to live under the guise of a repulsive animal or person. The most common way of breaking the spell is with a kiss on the lips. But it may also be broken by lying down with, caressing or treating the loathsome being kindly. Contrarily, the spell may be broken by a violent act. In one old English tale, the frog asks the young girl to chop off his head with an ax. As soon as she does, a handsome prince appears: "…the lassie brought the ax, and chopped off the frog's head, as instructed, and no sooner was that done than he started up the bonniest young prince that ever was seen…"

In the Brothers Grimm's version, it is only when the princess throws the frog against the wall that he recovers his human form.

According to Maria Tatar in her book THE HARD FACTS OF THE GRIMMS' FAIRY TALES, tenderness and violence are intertwined in these stories: "The princess in the Grimms' version of 'The Frog King' may simply be displaying her spontaneous reaction to the unending importunities of a 'disgusting frog' when she hurls him against the wall, but she may also have behind her act the weight of folkloric traditions that require an act of physical violence for love to flourish in its most human and humane form."

Bettelheim suggests that these tales reflect the moment of surprise and violence in which we recognize that what we consider to be bestial and repulsive in ourselves and others is, in fact, revealed as the source of human happiness.

The version that appears in this book is based on the Brothers Grimm's version, except for two differences:

• The requests the frog makes of the princess take place during a single night in the Grimm's tale. But English versions refer to three consecutive nights during which the frog makes his demands, and we preferred the repetition.

• At the end of the tale, the Brothers Grimm introduce a loyal servant of the bewitched prince, Iron Henry, who was given his nickname because he had three iron bands laid around his heart to prevent it from bursting with sadness after his master was changed into a frog. The Iron Henry character and episode have not been included because they distract from the tale's central theme, namely the struggle between duty and pleasure and the relationship between the princess and the bewitched prince.

The Three Feathers

There are many folktales in which the older brothers make fun of the youngest brother, who is either not as clever or as suave as they are. They call him names and make him feel inferior. The teasing intensifies when they are put to the test by their parents. In the end, however, it is always the youngest — the fool — who comes out as the winner or as the one who is best able to carry out the tasks assigned to him.

According to Bettelheim, "The Three Feathers" is a tale that gives children a feeling of security. However intelligent children are, they are faced with a complex, unknown world, which can be frightening. Seeing that a character others call a fool manages to do things his elders are incapable of is reassuring for children, and allows them to believe that they, too, will be able to take on seemingly impossible challenges in life.

It is interesting to note that the title chosen for this tale comes from a relatively irrelevant detail, namely the feathers the father blows into the air to see which direction his sons will take. In some Slavic versions, the king shoots three arrows and each son must follow one of the arrows. This is destiny as decided by chance. It is also important to point out that the feather that falls closest to home indicates the way to objects of worth. This is also a recurring motif in folktales. Frequently what we are looking for, even the most sought-after treasure, is to be found close at hand, perhaps within ourselves. Many travelers who journey far and wide looking for treasure return home empty-handed only to find it was there in their own homes all the time.

The version that appears in this book is based on the tale

collected by the Brothers Grimm and on a few Spanish-language variants.

BEARSKIN

This story, one of the least well known among the more than two hundred tales published by the Brothers Grimm, touches on a popular theme in folktales — the pact made with the devil and the way in which, through his ingeniousness, a peasant or penniless man can outwit the lord of the underworld. In the case of "Bearskin," the protagonist is a poor soldier who triumphs over the "elegant gentleman wearing a long, green dresscoat," with the ugly tail and frightening cloven hoof.

A character's obligation to wear an animal's skin harkens back to Perrault's story "Donkeyskin" and to "Thousand-Furs" by the Brothers Grimm. But all similarities end there. The soldier in "Bearskin" abides by his pact with the devil despite the seemingly impossible nature of his task — having to spend seven years wearing a bear's skin and never bathing or cutting his hair or nails. His tenacity is rewarded with great riches and he finds true love.

The plot's resolution is a motif common to other tales, namely the youngest daughter's sacrifice in agreeing to marry a monster, in this case Bearskin, in order to keep her father's promise. The soldier promises to return for his fiancée three years later, which is when his pact with the devil runs out. On his return, rid of his frightful appearance, he does not announce who he is immediately — another common motif in romance stories and traditional tales — until he has seen for himself the young girl's loyalty.

The version that appears here is based on the Brothers Grimm's tale.

BIBLIOGRAPHY

Almodóvar, Antonio Rodríguez. CUENTOS AL AMOR DE LA LUMBRE
(Vol. I y II). Madrid: Ediciones Generales Anaya, 1998-1999.

Bettelheim, Bruno. THE USES OF ENCHANTMENT: THE MEANING AND
IMPORTANCE OF FAIRY TALES. New York: Alfred A. Knopf, 1976.

—— BRUNO BETTELHEIM PRESENTA LOS CUENTOS DE PERRAULT. Barcelona:
Editorial Crítica, 1980.

Grimm, J. and W. CUENTOS DE NIÑOS Y DEL HOGAR. Madrid:
Ediciones Generales Anaya, 1985.

Opie, Iona and Peter. THE CLASSIC FAIRY TALES. London: Granada
Publishing Limited, 1980.

Perrault, Charles. CONTES DE PERRAULT. Paris: Garnier, 1967.

——PERRAULT'S FAIRY TALES, WITH THIRTY-FOUR FULL-PAGE ILLUSTRATIONS BY
GUSTAVE DORÉ. New York: Dover Publications, 1969.

Tatar, Maria. THE HARD FACTS OF THE GRIMMS' FAIRY TALES. Princeton,
New Jersey: Princeton University Press, 1987.

Thompson, Stith. THE FOLKTALE. Berkeley and Los Angeles:
University of California Press, 1977.

Zipes, Jack. THE GREAT FAIRY TALE TRADITION: FROM STRAPAROLA AND
BASILE TO THE BROTHERS GRIMM. New York, London: W.W.
Norton & Company, 2001.

I